Kimiko

Love is what makes
the world go round

Love can make you
or
Love can break you

J. D. Logue

KIMIKO

iUniverse books may be ordered through booksellers or by contacting:

iUniverse
1663 Liberty Drive
Bloomington, IN 47403
www.iuniverse.com
1-800-Authors (1-800-288-4677)

ISBN: 978-1-5320-7944-3 (sc)
ISBN: 978-1-5320-7945-0 (e)

Print information available on the last page.

iUniverse rev. date: 07/29/2019

Prologue

IN the fifties with the occupation of Japan, The Korean war in full swing. A large number of United States Armed Forces. Absence from home for the first time. Youthful young men, not having experience in the far Eastern ways of life, Some of these (G. I.) not knowing lust from love. Married women from the Eastern Rim counties. Now the G I's that was in love and the women was also in love. The marriage lived on for a life time!

However the marriage of lost is the only ones we hear about. The mothers of our lusting men were infuriated.

Furiously these mothers took pin in hand. Thousands of infuriated mothers sent letters to their United States Senators express their dislikes. When the Senators begins receiving voters letters about their boys, The infuriated mothers relaying with great grief and sorrow, their son's marriage breaking up, going through divorces. What about the children who keeps them? The wife wants to return to their home counties taking the children. The US Senate stated "We have to put a stop to this!" The Uniform Code of Military Justice (U. C. M. J.) The Senate can and did vote in a new law in.

(UCMJ) to stop the marriages between these G. I. and un-American women. Kimiko and Jim where swept up in the turmoil this extremely agitated condition. Back in the old days I don't know; say before WORLD WAR one or even before that. One would have to receive permission (Formal consent from your Commanding Officer) before marriage. Jim did request consent to marry a Japanese national. He received formal consent from his Commanding Officer; A full bird navy Caption of the United States Ship "Jupiter." After they where married for some time. It come to light they (Kim & Jim) where to apply and receive consent from WEST PACIFIC COMMAND; (WESPAC). At the time Kim and Jim where married Kimiko was 22 years old, Jim was 27 years old. Now you would think the two of them was old enough to inter into marriage without Legislation of the United States Senate.

Jim stated "To all you mother, Command officer, U.S. Senators; whoever thinks they know what is best for their fellowman, and imposes their way of thinking upon his/her rights. Hindering them in their pursuit of happiness!

That's wrong as HELL."

Kim and Jim's Marriage has listed fifty years now hopefully for fifty more. Kim said "My sailor; speak to me in English fifty years ago and he is still full of it right up to his eye balls"

We do hope you enjoy our narration of this true life story.

This story is based on true experiences of two individuals named KIM AND JIM.

It's all true, it all happen only names and dates have changed in some cases; it took place in.

California, Kansas, Oklahoma, Texas, and Washington state and Washington D. C.

In countries like China, Japan, Korea, Philippines, Vietnam and Cuba.

From 1950 to 2002 centered on a sailor named Jim.

The saga unfolds when he meets an attractive Japanese woman named Kimiko while stationed overseas.

The two discover a mutual attraction for each other.

But find that there is an unspoken code of racism blocking their desire to marry.

An evocative sequence of event ensues as Jim realizes that he will be incomplete without Kimiko.

They decide to marry despite the tension it may cause.

Fast paced events, action and tender climax combine to render an original and richly detailed romance.

Chapter One

From Kimiko

The big red rooster was crowing and crowing. He was next door in the neighbor's back yard. His crowing had awakened Jim. He looked at the clock that sits on the night stand next to the bed. 0610 hours February 12, 2002.As he lay there in bed, looking up at the pastel yellow ceiling. The morning sun's thin beams of light doing a little dance across the ceiling. The window was ajar permeating a cool breeze to seep through, making the light rose drapes to move and the beam of sun light to dance.

Sleepy he bent over kissing the woman next to him awake. Saying "get up! My wife will be home anytime now". The woman lazily turning over on her side with her back to him, pulling the bed covers up over her head. Saying "Look Jimmy boy thus is not Kansas there are no live stock to tend to, so go away; I need my sleep". "Are you going to sleep all day? Lyn and Bob will be here this afternoon" was Jim's reply. Lyn was the first and only daughter. Form under the bed covers, "the four grandchildren and the long drive up here Lyn and Bob will sleep well tonight". Kim was saying as Jim went into the kitchen preparing to make coffee. She heard the knocking about of pots and pans. The coffee pot being filled with water. "O" shit he making coffee. As she jump up putting on her house robe, as she run for the kitchen. "Jim you are the eater, I'm the cook! Now you know that. So go out and sit down, I'll have your coffee in know time". He walked out the front door. After he walked down the driveway/ Retrieving the paper turning back he seen the car shed. Thinking to himself is (Mr. No up?) Mr. No was the first son J. R. he don't have a pot, or a window to throw it out!

He lives up over the car shed in two small rooms. He's positively Mr. No; No rent, no car, no house, no wife, no job, no children. Hell he don't even have a pet!

Jim came back into the kitchen. Kim had the coffee and toast with jam on the side. They sit looking out the back window at the garden. Kim knew Jim was angry with J. R. for leaving the navy after doing nine and a half years. Just ten more he could have retired. She went over next to him sit down beside him at the kitchen nook table. Taking his hand into hers and squeezing it. That was Kim's way of saying; I love you and whatever comes. It will be all right. She said "it won't be too bad having seven grandchildren under foot for the weekend. Andrew the baby of the family, him and his wife Joann with the three children from hell, will be coming over from Klamath Falls for the party. It's been 48 years of blissful marriage for Kim and Jim. It was just after twelve O'clock when a auto come up the driveway it was Joann and Andrew with the three brats. Jim letting out his breath and going to the front door. Calling out "HAY; my three little hell raiser, how my three brats today". They run from the auto and jumping onto Grandpa. "Grandpa; Grandpa we have not seen you in a long time". The dog hearing the children coming. Run out his dog door across the back into the car shed and under the auto, he stay under their tell it's time to eat. Jim and Andrew stopped in the kitchen. Andrew say hello to his mother they received a cup of Kim's good coffee, She disposed of Jim's coffee right away.

To keep the cat or dog from dieing off. If they was to get some im said "Now dad you and Andrew keep a eye on the children and don't let them run up and down the stairway". "Hell no we don't wont to wake J. R. he has been a sleep 16 hours bow that's out of a 24 hour day" Jim said. As the two of them went out the back door. Kim said to Joann "I don't know what to do with them two (J. R. and Dad). They are like two cats and dogs at each other all the time. Jim said "J. R, is lower than whale shit, and that at the bottom of the sea". Kim going to the kitchen sink running water over the vegetable and placing the vegetable in a cooking pot and placing the cover on as she sat the pot on the stove. As Joann removed items from the table and preparing to set the table for dinner. Andrew and Jim setting under the large apple tree. As they looked after the children as they run around the back yard. Andrew asking about the garden. Jim said "the new hydro phonics system was working very nicely, the solar energy package is working out. When I get it all together it should be nice". The children are running up and the steps. Jim was laughing for he knew they would wake up J. R. It was around 1:00 p.m., and way past time for J. R. to be up and about. So Jim just set back and let the kids run up and down the stairs. Andrew drinks all his coffee run water from the outside tap, set the cup on the drain board. Returning to where Jim was setting; under the large apple tree. Jim asking how's your new job, how do you like being the manager? Andrew stated it was all new but things are looking up. The pay was much better. Plus a dollar will go father in Oregon than in California. The rain takes a little getting to know how to get around in but the family likes it here in Oregon. Will that is nice.

Jim said Yes Kim and I just love it up here can't see leaving in California with all that traffic. We have a little money and all the time in the world, to go where every we like to go when were was in Kansas, Kim and I had the time. But the weather was hot in the summer and to cold in the winner, not like here in Oregon. Jr. came out of his room laughing and running after the brats. Then he come down and set down under the big apple tree, be side Jim. Asking Andrew "how you like being the manager of a new store. The family how they like there new home?"Jim stood up going into the back door, went over to the kitchen sink after running water into the cup he turned it upside-down setting the cup on the sink drain board. Went into the living room, looking out the window at the driveway he seen Lyn and Bob driving into the driveway. As they come walking up the drive the children was all in line with Lyn and Bob walking in back, In respect for their mother and father, they come in the front door. Jim spoke to the the children as they come ibto the house, Lyn ask "where's mom and how have you been? You're looking good."Bob and Jim said their hellos as they went in the front door. Bob stopped in the kitchen to say hello to Kim and Joann as they went out into the back yard. All the men sat under the large apple tree, having ice tea or coffee. Andrew had just stop smoking said he needed some gum this stopping smoking is for the birds. Some times I'm about to go nuts, but as long as I'm doing. But when I'm sitting around not doing anything that is what drives me nuts. Kim calling out the back door "come and get it". She turned and disappeared back in the house. The children come running from every direction.

After dinner and the table were cleaned up, the family had sat down to watch TV and play family games. The small dog came out from under the car, where he been hiding all afternoon. Tyler, the rat dog, short haired Chihuahua goes to the back door peaking through his dog door to see if all the children were in the other room. Not seeing any children, he slowly went through into the kitchen, going to his water first and then he eats, and more water. After that slowly crossed the room looking to see where the children were at he went to J. R. to be picked up. J. R. asking where have you been all day? One of Andrew's children comes over to play with the dog. Tyler growls at her, the small girl backed away. About that time Kim and Jim went out the front door and down the driveway. Hand-in-hand they walked on the side of the road. Lyn and Bob watched from the window, arm in arm. Lyn asked do you think we will be in love like they are when we reached their age?" Bob said "We can only hope." The old couple on the street coming to the corner turning on to the main road disappeared from their view. The old couple slowly walked on up the road, as they come to the top of the hill they could see the Pacific Ocean reaching out as far as the eye can see. "Kim my beautiful young Japanese beauty." Jim was thinking to himself.

In his mind's eye seeing the most beautiful Japanese woman in all of Japan, her long black hair; has turned to silver and her face had age lines and she walks a little slower. However her love for her old sailor boy had not wavered over the years. If one would believe in love at first sight then one could know what was in her heart all the years they have been together. Jim also having a hart full of love for his Kimiko. Now time had taken its toll on this sailor.

They are hand-in-hand as the sun vanishes into the golden Pacific Ocean. The old man's mind wonder's back over the years to the days of their youth.

A young woman in Japan.

Jim was thinking about, how GOD had bless this old sailor. A loving wife; and their family. Yes the loving time we had in Japan, and in Texas, Oklahoma, Kansas, New Mexico, California and here in Oregon.

How can one say with a wife like Kimiko, no man has the right to be so blessed with overwhelming joy and happiness?

With just a wink of the eye, the years just fly by. The old man's mind wonders the years of lone ago back to youth full times. Would the happiest time be the times in Japan; the first time in the hot bath. Or in Texas where our first child was concede; here in Oregon state in our golden years of life.

(THE GOLDEN YEARS HAS COME AT LIST)
I cannot See; I cannot Pee; I cannot chew; I cannot Screw; Hearing stinks; Memory shrinks; Gone my sense of smell; Look like hell.
Those Golden Years Have come at list.
THOSE GOLDEN YEARS CAN KISS MY ASS.

As I recalled, it was in 1950; when the North KOREAN TROOPS invaded South Korea. Jimmy boy back in Kansas was going in a run, not knowing where he was running to however, He was in a full out to get there. It didn't take a genius to come to the concession if this poor old county boy from the western planes of Kansas don't chain his behavior he will end up in the Army, I'm just what the Army was looking for at that time right out of college and just what the Army was looking for. I went to Enid, Oklahoma and joined the United States Navy, October 16, 1950. After bases training I received my orders to naval air station in Washington state. Before reporting for duty I had two weeks I went back home to Kansas that was two weeks of hell night in one. One night after all the beer halls had closed the Hanes brothers and I stopped by Pets the (moon/ shiner) place. Pet made the best malt liquor in Kansas, We all had more than we needed.

About 3:00 AM one of the brothers was going to drive his new Ford through the house, he tipped the vehicle over. I had two weeks of that! I drove my three window 1940 Ford coup to Washington and checked in for more schooling, mote training, Air crewmen survival school. Out on the shooting rang; the Navy found out two things. I can out talk and shoot anyone on Whidbey Island. The combination the Navy made me an instructor on small bore arms. The Browning automatic rifle

(B. A. R.). The .45 caliber Thompson (The old Timmy gun). The .38 police special. The one I liked was the 1911 army colt .45 semi-automatic. I had more time off duty than I did money. At first I would drive into the small town of Oak Harbor, it was like being on the Air Station. One weekend one of the other instructors ask if I would like to come with him to Bellingham. The drive through the country side along the Puget Sound was nice. John said he had a date for me if I'd like. I agreed to participate in this blind date. As it turned out the girl was about Twenty-five and around twenty pounds overweight and dumb as dirt. I for the life of me did not think I would turn down a woman that you have to put a pork chop around her neck to get the dog to play with her. This one was the biggest turn off I had ever come across. The next day was Sunday I went to Sunday School and church. Stopping at one of Bellingham good restaurant for dinner, and proceed back to my room. I had Monday off know one schedule for the day. I drove over to the State University, stop at the college coffee shop. I said to a student. Hay how's it going. I attended Kansas state. How do you like it here? He said "man I love it here three female forever male and I'm trying to get more than my sheer if I can so far I'm doing all right

He would say "Look at that, or did you see that one over their". After a time looking at the females, two young women set down at the table with us. John did the honors stating "Ms. Pam I would like to introduce you to Jim. Jim; Pam Jennifer this is Jim. Jim this is Jennifer". I'm looking at the door at a very tall red headed woman coming through the door, walking to our table. She was six foot 5 or 6. John seen me looking at her. He said no, that one don't go out". Ginger is on the college basketball team. All she can think about is basketball. After our small group had said there piece. Ginger was next to me at the table. I asked her out. She looked down at me and said "NO THANK YOU!" You know I'm not going to stop at that small no. I was thinking think* ing how I would like to get that big red headed woman in bed. One of the girls related we have to go it's almost 5:30 the bus will be here we'll have to run for it. I said "I have my car and I'm going down town. Where you going?" Jennifer said we are at the(Y. W. C. A.) downtown just off Broadway 2 1/2 blocks. You just around the corner from where I'm at. Ginger said "you two can go on if you would like to. I'm going to take the bus." When we come to my car three young lacies said we can not all fit in that small coupe! Yes we can I have had 13 girls in my little Ford coupe before so step in, I turn the key and the motor come alive the three were inside and the door closed and we were off. The four of us arrived at the (Y) as I turned off Broadway I ask Ginger for her phone number. No way she said. Will how am I going to call you to ask you out. I'm not handing out my phone number to you or anyone so for get it!

The other two young ladies was laughing at me. One said see Ginger if you don't permit him to phone, he's going to walk funny the rest of his life. Ginger was laughing by now. With a half a smile she took my hand and turning it over wrote her name and phone number on the inside of my hand. As the weeks passed by I enjoyed her company; and she got to enjoy mine. I have successfully succeeded in coming acquainted with a nice college student. Now the Y. W. C, A. would lock the exterior doors at 12. Midnight and if you ring the doorbell they would write a letter to your parents, about you being out after midnight. The first time Ginger got lock out, she would not come up to my room. Now my 1940 Ford coupe is just too small to sleep in. After being locked out two or three more times and sleeping in that small coupe. Big red come to my room, the first night, I was the gentleman and stayed on the floor. The next time a week later I went to bed and made love over and over, Ginger was a very tall woman with long legs, small breast 38A I would say. She was a good lover with all the right moves; and good timing. This one Friday night we in my room on the bed, I have my hands under her blouse playing with her maple, watching television. We helped each other out of our clothing, she started performing oral sex that started a long weekend after that every time I would have time off we would go to the room, I don't know if she or I like it more in the hot and sweaty afternoons in that small room. Sundays we'd go to Sunday school after the service we would go to a nice restaurant for Sunday dinner. Then back to the room for some afternoon loving. We would go out dancing, Ginger was six foot 5 or 6 inches tall, red hair; green eyes. When we dance I can lay my head on her breast.

Then I received my orders to sea duty (What a downer). I'm to report to the first ship I've ever seen or been on. The United States Ship Jupiter (AVS-8) she was first commission the Flying Cloud in 1939. a old liberty ship WW-2. When I arrived in Alameda California it was cold and looked like it was going to rain. As I stopped at the Naval Air Station southgate I ask the jarhead where can I find the Jupiter theMarine said first stop sign turn left 1 1/2 miles from here. As I was driving I could see three or four raindrops on my window. I stopped at the stop sign I seen the ships. As I come closer to the dock I seen the Jupiter berth between two other ships. The ships were old and in need of repair done on them. Iturn into the parking lot and parked my little Ford coupe. Walking out on the dock, the wharf had ships on both sides I seen in two foot black letters (U, S. S. Jupiter under that it read in one foot letters United States Navy.

As I come near the gangway looking back over the water one can see the water front of San Francisco. The water seem alive with the glow from the opposite shore sparking light that dance on the waves.

I stared; a bit hypnotize by the random bouncing of the small waves tapping the pier. A rainbow shimmering off the water giving signs of fuel that leak from one of the ships. All the color sitting intermittent sparking lights. Damn; this water is really polluted. A distant thrumming it's a steady sounding in one tone. A long with the attendant odor of diesel exhaust was in the evening breeze. That diesel powered a generators supplying the needed power to keep the Jupiter's lights running.

A cold impersonal feeling come over me; the twinkling lights from the water was just an observable fact or nature.

The flickering of the small lights generates a warm feeling for no reason.

Turning back to the ship, the one I'll spin two years of my life on. As I lifted my sea/bag upon my shoulder and crossing the wharf and as I stepped up on the gangway; the question come to mind (what the hell has this country boy gotten him self into) Liken onto Daniel in the lions den.

I come to the top of the gangway and just before I stepped onto the Jupiter I salute the colors; and turning to the officer of the quarter deck. Salute the officer of the day. "I request permission to come aboard; Sir."

The officer of the day replied "Permission granted welcome aboard". The master of arms showed me to my quarter. The next day I was upon deck, it was one of those warm spring days. The sunrise had been five minute ago and the officer of the deck was not 100 percent alert as the night lights was on. The white Nancy light at the top of the masts, and the red anti/collision lights were burning. The water inside the bay had almost perfect smoothness, about it. In the emerging light of day giving off a bronze colored sky not yet the blue color of day. Which will be an intense blue, is just a little dulled by the night. The night that understand it must yield; as the sun inching its way over the East Oakland foothills. The red wine of sunlight run out over the sky turned red to blue the light does not hurt ones eyes.

A truck comes to a stop and some sailors milling around the back to unload the needy supplies. On the main deck their were others moving about so the day began. Later on I found out some of Jupiter operation. Their are 16 officers and 265 men on board. The officers mess will be opening soon and I'll meet the people I'll know if you pass gas ten other people will know it.

I was the low man on the Jupiter the new ensign.

At 0630 hours west coast time I went into the offices mess. After coffee I was shown the inter working of the Jupiter by T. J. another low life ensign. The long day slowly comes to a end. I was standing on the wharf looking for a hint about the Jupiter. My thoughts was I don't know anymore about her then I did the day before. When I was standing looking up at this large ship.

I walked to the end of the dock, so I can use the payphone. I made two phone calls, one to my home in Kansas. Telling my parents I had arrived all right. The other call was to Bellingham, Washington; Ginger was not in school at this time she would be at the Y. W. C. A. she will be in the dorm. The Y operator ring her room. After the small talk was over, I ask Ginger to fly down to San Francisco for the week end. We can see San Francisco like young couples are intended to see the city of love together.

Ginger said "I'd love to fly down to San Francisco and make love to you and see San Francisco with you. But I can't do it for many reasons. I just can't do it, my life is planned and you can't be in it. So don't telephone me anymore we are yesterday news, goodbye forever." The telephone went silent. Now "isn't this a kick in the ass!" After I replace the receiver. I preceded to the parking lot. I set in my car for some time thinking about Ginger and Washington. Saying to myself hay what the hell. I have not lost a thing. I received better than I gave. I received a lot of loving, good sex. It's over I have my freedom. Look out San Francisco here I come. With one hand on the steering wheel the other on my self. I went out the gate and over to Harrison street and into Oakland turning right onto East 14th street past the Alameda County courthouse and lake Mead. Stopping at the Grand Prix have a beer checking out the young female customers there were one or two nice looking ladies their. I went outside it was dark, I got in my car and proceeded on out East 14th street.

I stopped at 83rd Avenue. There is a drugstore where a friend of mine used to sale newspapers after school when I was in San Leandro high school. Most of the businesses were closed up and the owners moved away. The old drugstore had removed their ice cream and soda bar. There was a new chemists at the window I asked him if he knew the old man that used to work here. He said "yes he is in the back." The old man come to the front and we spoke about the yesteryear and the other high school boys that used to hang around here. After a time he went back to work. I got in the car and continued on out East 14th. street to Callan Ave. Stopping at my aunts house, we visited for over a half-hour. I said "Anti I have to go on back to my ship and get some sleep, I have a big day tomorrow." After that I preceded over to MacArthur Boulevard and back to Alameda and the Jupiter. In a large city like the East Bay, one can be forgotten in a New York minute.

I come on board in 1950 that means it will be 1952 or 53; teal my sea duty is completed. We made port of call in the Philippines, China, Japan and Korea, on our first cruise. This is to show you just how slow the Jupiter was. I'm marking the days off on a calendar. Over 90 days after the two weeks of war games out of Hawaii and then on to Japan, arrived in Yokoska Navy Station on the big island of Honshu after a fortnight we sailed into the inland sea of Japan. Stopping two nights at Iwakuni. After that; back on the inland sea of Japan, the Jupiter pass through the Shimonsek straits. Into to sea of Japan off the south coach of Korea. We past this one very small island of Ullung more than one time. The Jupiter would go up the coast north to NaJin; and back to PuSon one time we stopped at PoHangDong. That's how she got her name.

(GALLOPING GHOST OF THE KOREAN COAST)

Now the Navy with all their wisdom comes up with a new stupid plan.

Put the Jupiter in near the coastline say around 15 miles out.

The north Korean can and will shoot at the Jupiter, spotting for the mighty MO the U. S. S. Missouri battleship (BB-63).

She is out at sea 15 to 20 miles. Stop and think the North Korean gun five miles in land fifteen miles out to sea to the Jupiter and twenty miles on to the mighty MO. that's 5+15+20 = forty miles away those big 16 inch guns can hit a fly in the ass. The sound of those 16 inch bullets going over the Jupiter whistling was all you can hear. Then you see the mountain explode and disappear. Man! Now that was something this county boy had never ever seen before. The Jupiter going stateside back to Alameda, California. The old Flying Cloud was underway come hell or high water. This one man by the name of T. J. Harvey from Tacoma, Washington. We pulled liberty in the Philippines, China, and in Japan. so I'm knowledgeable of what T. J. looked like I have never seen him without a beard. I'm going going down this hallway when this young man said "how you doing Jim ?" I don't know this little you know what! I stopped him and ask "Just what the hell is the big idea of addressing me in that manner," The young man said" Hell after I got you out of all that trouble in Shanghai,

I assumed I would have the right." O shit it's T. J. he had cut his beard off. He stated "No one on the ship know who I am". You remember we are in the middle of the ocean. Hay LTJG Bobby Blackbird is the (O. O. D.): on the officer of the day. So T. J. and I preceded to the O. O. D office as I'm setting down I said "Hi Bobby; I have a new man checking in for duty." (Now here we are 2000 miles a way from any port). A new man checking on board?? Now come on Bobby!!

Blackbird ask "your name Al E. Norman Your rank T. J. said LTJG sir!

Now this nut is logging all of this into the official ships log.

We did not get into trouble over that. The C. O. did say do not do it any more.

Up on arriving in Alameda Air Station T. J. received his orders transferring off the Jupiter, good for him. After departing Alameda was war games off Hawaii and then onto (WESPAC). One night will off the Aleution Islands we were will out to sea. I seen Auroras Borealis lights; It would be most difficult to tale you about them they are beautiful. It's like the first time you see a whale come up all the way out of the water, or a school of dolphins swimming with the ship. That is what makes a sailor walk with a swagger.

He knows he has been there and seen it for himself. Knowing; not one of you land lovers never will! The replacement for T. J. come aboard at Alameda his name was Dees from Houston, Texas he was (L T). This one afternoon in Japan he asked if I would go with him to have dinner in town. We ended up night club hoping. The next day before I ever opened my eyes I knew I was in deep DO-DO. I did not know were I was but were ever it is. It's not on the Jupiter. The sun was in my eyes and I don't have a porthole around me on the Jupiter Dees was in the room next door I got him up, asking where are we. He replied I was hoping you knew. I went outside and it was colder then my girls heart. Ice and snow everywhere. There was no other building or cars. There was no roads that's was why no cars. We are out where the hoot owls make love to the chickens. In Hong Kong we would have to take a water taxi into the city. They was all kinds of tailor shops they serve beer and other alcohol as they take your order for what ever ? You would leave your name and your clothing be done to be picked up the next day. That day never comes. I would use names like I. W. Hopper or J. C. Penny as I down beer after beer. How ever I never got any clothing. This one time I said my name was Robert E. Lee. The Chinese in the shop said "you not Chinese, your right name if you please; please write me." So I did Mr. I. W. Hopper III.

The fortnight we were in Hong Kong, Mary's side cleaner and her women painted the ship for her pay was the garbage.

Hong Kong Mary was crazy like a fox. It was about 12 years or so Hong Kong Mary was on 29/29 TV features one of the wealthiest women in Hong Kong.

Korea 0600 hours off PoHngDong; the U. S. S. Missouri battleship BB-63 firing her large 16 inch guns; about ever 19 seconds she would lob one over the Jupiter. Ships of United Nations were shooting at the beach for hours. On board the Jupiter the landing party was going over the side down into the landing craft. United with other landing craft of the United Nations. 0645 hours made their run for the beach.

Jim was hump over, squatting down on his heels. With his Browning Automatic rifle (B A R) between his legs. With his head down he was thinking, would you just look at me. I enlisted into the Navy just so I would not have to do this. I'm not a jar-head (U S M C). So what the hell am I doing here in the bottom of this landing craft, I'm in the Navy I am to stay on the ship, not on a landing party. Just look a round and you'll see I'm the smallest one here and they gave me the biggest gun in the landing craft. I have two men to help bring the ammunition. This old girl needs 850 rounds a minute on high, Jim turn the selector to slow that is 759 rounds per minute. Each ammunition man has his M-1 and 4400 rounds for Jim gun he had 520 rounds himself. All in all that was 11minutes of shooting time. The lead man shouting loudly, over the boat motor "load and lock" Jim worked the slide putting the BAR on safety. He stated to the two ammunition men stay near me. I need ammunition ever one here needs the cover this Browning Automatic rifle will give so stay nearby.

The front door of the landing craft drop open; all hell broke loose!

Jim used over 1000 rounds of ammunition crossing the beach.

Running and shooting they crossed the beach. Jim and the two ammunition men lay on there backs side-by-side. Jim rolling over got to his knees looking over the top of the small sanded hill, he seen north Korean army machine cutting down men as they departed there landing craft. It was the second wave of United Nations forces coming ashore. Jim pulling the BAR to his shoulder lining up on the first machine gun shot 19 rounds new clap and shooting the second machine gun nest, running his finger foreword the release button, the clap fall out the ammunition man replacing it Jim shot machine gun three and the four the B A R was so hot they needed to stop before the barrel become unusable. But how can he stop the north Korean machine gunners wee killing the scond wave of United Nations men. "Use go" as they run along to get to a better place.

They began to receive rifle fire from the top of a cliff top which was about 4or5 feet high. But he raise the Browning over the top of the cliff and shot 20 rounds, new clip and shooting 20 more rounds to the other side and new clip. Jim asking how much ammunition do we have ammunition man #1 said he was out, the other man said he had 800 rounds. Give it to me and you two go back and get more ammunition, Go now as he fired two more clips to keep the north Korean heads down. He fire 3 or 4 rounds at a time. The Browning was to quick he could not issue just one around at a time his finger to reacted was to slow.

12 American army and five south Korean come up. The sergeant ask "What the hell is the Navy doing out here ?" The two ammunition men returned, "we have 8,000 rounds" Jim saying "all right it's ass kicking time". Jim got to his feet running "if it moves I'm going to shoot it". Running Jim was using ammunition like it was going out of style. Running as fast as they can he stopped cold turning to his right; shooting the hell out of the side of the hill. It was a North Korean bunker the soldiers come running out and the Browning Automatic Rifle cut them down as they ran. It must have been an ammunition bunker it exploded fire and smoke shot into the air.

The Jupiter travels south to the land of source of the sun (Nippon) four islands make up the part of Japan. Up on arrival we stopped at Sasebo on the southern Island.

I did not like Japanese beer so the list bar I was in was in the city of Sasebo. The Jupiter departed Sasebo going in a southern duration then east past the Island of Kyushu into the inland sea of Japan past the island of Shikoku with in the inland sea of Japan and on in to Yokosuka.

I have cut out using cigarette, whisky and beer. You know a sailor will never see the beauty of Japan all he will see is the inside of a bar.

Two shipmates and I rented a quaint old fashion 100 % percent Japanese house up on a hill over looking the bay. It was older and bigger than the three of us needed. The house was in a L shape with a large Japanese flower garden, sidewalks and a fish pond and wooden benches to set on in the afternoon and look at the sun go down. A nice p[ace to enjoy a good after dinner smoke or a class of brandy. The house had four bedrooms with one large room that made up the other half of the L it was about 50 x 65 ft. We had large eat in kitchen plus a dining room. 'O' the hot bath, the bath is not for washing self. No you wash off with soap and water after you shower then you may proceed to the hot bath the one we had was about 8x12 foot and hotter than hell.

Men, women and children attend at the same time.

There was no shamefulness. The bathtub we had could accommodate a round eight at one time. Strict traditional rules, with no embarrassment.

The floors of the house are made of straw called tatami mates.

Between rooms the doors are covered with rice paper screens. The large room and two of the bedrooms over look the garden.

The three of us pay $25 each making the rent $75. a month.

That pays the rent and for a old man and his wife; to keep the grounds and cook for us. That come to 27375 yen (365 yen to one dollar) at that time.

In Japan on a cold night the Japanese style ever one get up under a big quilt, about like two king-size quilts stitched together.

Up next to the **HIBACHI POT** That is also under the quilt.

The day we moved into the house, the Jupiter was having an inspection that morning in honor of the United Nations.

The uniform of the day was full dress whites with large metals, and all of the assessors. The whole nine yards. There was more United Nation combative countries and political groups from more nation's than I can name. The United States Navy command task force 77 inside the bay Aircraft carriers four American two United Kingdom and other surface ships and submarines. On the aircraft carriers flight deck had aircraft like the F 9 F panther, F4 corsair, AD5 sky readers and the new F2H banshee.

Ships from all of the United Nations that was assembly was represented that morning.

It was mid afternoon it was over and the taxi comes to the ship.

to take the three of us up the hill. If you ever wondered what ever happen to all of them Japanese Kamikaze pilots after the war was over.

I can tale you; they all become taxi drivers.

When the taxi drop us off at the end of the side street. I was half blinded by the sunlight.

As the three of us walked up the small rise going to the house and just before going through the gate I looked up at the end of the street their I seen a most beautiful young woman coming out and turning to secure the gate that run across the end of the street and walking in my direction.

Entering into the courtyard the two old people was there to greet us bowing in respect of their new employers.I was polite with a small bow in respect of our new employees Stating it is nice of you to welcome us in to our new home.

Please excuse me now I must chain out of this uniform.

19

Going in to the house I removed my shoes went into my room and out of that white uniform. Went in took a shower then into the hot bath to relax, closing my eyes "MAKE THE WORLD GO AWAY" The next day we met some of our new neighbors.

When a neighbor would come to the house. The cook/ housekeeper woman would bow her head on the floor would take 15 minutes just to enter the house. It's all come from the old time honor and customs of Japanese honoring the visitor. From what I understand she is stating "Come set on my uncomforable pillow if I had a better one I would offer it to you. Please accept my most humble apology" that about what said to your visitor up on their arrival. This is passed down from generation to generation.

In three weeks the new was wore off. We are going site seeing so the three blind mice where off. Taking the bus we are off to see the beauty of Japan.

The bus the three of us was riding stopped at every street corner. That's all right we are not in a hurry for you know the bus will stop downtown.

WRONG it went right past the big bus stop, and right back up the hill. Waving and laughing and calling out the window to the young ladies we past. We got off the bus at the same bus stop we had started from. We are laughing at each other for being so damn dumb. The gardener seeing what happened.

Said in Japanese to the cook "go to the neighbors and bring back that young lady that can speak English. In a minute the cook had returned, With a very nice young lady, the cook said "She can speaks English two damn good I wager."

The woman was around twenty years old. Her hair was in a ponytail, a white cotton blouse and blue jeans.

She said hello my name is Kimiko.

She could speak English quite well like a English lady not like an American. It was the Kings English I did don't quite know what to think about that.

I said to Neil "I think that's quite nice." She spoke to the three of us stating : The old lady said you needed a translator and you would like to go to Yokohama is that correct?" I said yes that's correct; we need someone to show us what train and bus we have to we have to take to go to Yokohama.

Kimiko ask where do you want to go? I would like to be your translator and guide. However in Japan unmarried women need an escort before she is permitted to be accompanying of a unmarried man.

We would like to go today. Do you know of someone that can help? Maybe you might know someone that can escort you?

Now if this old country boy was reading the signs right what the lady was saying the escort is to keep the fox out of the chicken house!

I walked with her back to her house where, she come out with one grandmother and two aunts. So we ended up with three escorts.

Dees and Neil and my self. All seven of us got on the bus, Kimiko showed me the Japanese symbol for express bus. We arrived at the train station they call out the train destination in Japanese.

All the time I was in Japan I was never sure where I was going to arrive at. However most of the time I would end up where I wanted to go. All seven of us departed the train at the Yokohama station. We got two taxi to take us to the Ginza. For all of you round eyes; the Ginza is a shopping district nothing like our shipping malls. They have stores, restaurants, theaters and nightclubs. When we arrived at the Ginza Dee was strait away off to the nightclub. He come home with us that afternoon. However he stopped coming out to the house after that Neil walked along by him self off to the side of us. The three older women where happily pleased and enjoying taking pleasure in the open shops going here and there like children. We stopped in a nice restaurant to eat, that made the three escorts ever happy. Kimiko was nice to us show the Japanese symbolize for the bus and other signs to help us out as we would need to know them when we went off on our own.

We lift the Ginza late that afternoon. We got back to Yokosuka around 1800 hours (6:00 P. M.) When we got off the bus at our stop. I slipped a 5,000 yen note into Kimiko hand and thank her for showing us the way to go to Yokohama. As we parted at my gate ever one said there good nights and went on there way. Two days has past I have not seen Kimiko, Then one afternoon I was coming down off the bus. Ms. Kimiko Amato was going by the bus stop on her way home from the market place. As we walk she said "The three old ladies are telling ever one about going to Yokohama."

I ask her "How did you like going with us American? Maybe some of your friends that don't like American would stop being your friend." She replied "Friends like that I don't need. It was quiet pleasant, I enjoyed my self and I liked going with you." Looking down and half bowing in that Japanese style. We stop at my gate. I ask her in for coffee. She answers "No my mother will be expecting me home." As she turns to go she hesitates holding back in doubt, looking back over her shoulder she replied "Perhaps some other time."

In a vary soft and low voice all most in a whisper. With a one more half a bow she walk on up the street. I thought to myself, will ring my chimes baby you are looking nice walk up the street.

The next day the old man and the old woman (cook) were going at it. Hell's fire and brimstone!

The old man said to Nail and I "the Amato family was mad as hell at him. Kimiko is liking one of you an American sailor it's one of you two. That her father was mad at him for asking her to come over here to translate for us. Now for three or four days I though about this. Now Kimiko and I are walking from the bus stop to my front gate of my house ever week night.

If her father was so P. O. at us, he can't be to angry at her and I or he would put a stop to it. One weekends her father and my old gardener were in the garden just outside my window talking the drunk talk.

Japanese drunks are not like Americans, where they get light hearted and happy. While the Americans turn the other way.

After over an hour of this I went out to have it out with this old man.

I have in mind to resolve this objection of his little girl seeing a American sailor. Will it was not the sailor, but the American sailor he was angry about. Maybe two weeks has past I just see Kimiko when we are coming from the bus stop and running into one another meeting on the street. It was the time of the year that the evening was getting warmer. This one evening I had my hot bath and in my Japanese style men's kimono and geta geta sandals I was strolling leisurely in the yard and out into the garden where some of the flowers where begun to bud out.

23

I enjoy the closing of the day. As I stepped out of my gate to go out into the street, I'm securing the gate.

Kimiko and her mother and father, her brother and her sister-in-law, when they were walking by, Kimiko said "ho Jimmyson; come and go with us we are going to the hill top park". I said "no your father", Kimiko replied "O no it's all right father just now said he would like for you to come with us. We are just going to the hill top park." We are at the park we can look down and see the Jupiter at the dock.

Kimiko and I are strolling around the park talking small talk.

I said "I would like to see more and maybe go out some time."

You well have to ask father but I would like that.

Kimiko father was sitting like a judge he put out his hand for me to sit. Her father and I sit looking out over the bay.

He said in good English "would you like to call on my house one afternoon?"

I just looked at him for a good minute. Here her father is braking my chops and all this time and old you know what can speak English all the time.

You can see with one eye that he has the influence and the authority over his house.

I said to him; if I have your permission it would gave me grate pleasure. After the sun had sat and we are going back down the hill.

There was just one small item that know one told me about. You can't go down hill with geta geta on.

With out understanding how the geta geta is made and you have did it two or three times slowly. That is to prevent one from falling down the hill. Look out here comes the American head over tea cup!

By the time I got down the hill, that had broken the ice Kimiko Father was laughing his head off. Joyfully he said "will you are no quitter. But next time just take the geta geta off."

The next day Kimiko said I was invited for tea Sunday afternoon at 1700hours (5:00 P. M.) Now this old country boy has never been to a tea party before. I ask the old cook lady about what I was to do.

She said "all you do is to set down; don't talk; You do is just set and receive the cup of tea. Then turning in your hand little by little tell you have turned it one turn no more just one turn is all. Now you test it by tasting drinking a small quantity.

So Sunday come and I was on time jest about I left my house at 5:00.

Kimiko served the old time tea ceremony. That's the preparation and serving of tea following complicate and strict rules in the traditional Japanese ceremony.

Kimiko was beautiful in her kimono she had on.

We never made eye contact tell after the ceremony was over.

Kimiko mother and father lift the room after that.

I was hopping I had not got married or any thing like that with this tea ceremony.

Kimiko taking my hand in hers as we went out into her garden. Walking and talking; the time slips away from us.

Even though we were alone, we were not isolated.

If you recall the sliding doors with rice paper covering. You don't know who's on the other side of the paper screen, A mother or

A father? I ask if she would like to go out to a theater in Yokohama next Friday. Kimiko said "Yes I would like that, however you well have to ask my father for his permission." We had a good time in the garden that afternoon. The moon come up full and reflecting so bright you can see to read by. I departed about 9:00 o'clock that evening. The next day I was over to see Mr. Amato to ask his permission for me to take his daughter to the theater in Yokohama this next Friday. The old man was agreeable. However dear grandmother had escort duty. Friday we got a taxi to the train station we got off at Yokohama station. Where we went by taxi to the theater. I don't know what the hell we seen it was a Kabuki drama.

It was a floor show. Dear grandmother liked it more than Kimiko or I did. You can keep your theater Japanese or American. Motion pictures! That's what I call the theater. All was not lost, I enjoyed Kimiko's company. The way she has in looking at things; to see her side of things.

NOW THIS IS WHY YOU TIP TAXI DRIVERS

The driver stop at the lane going up to the five house where.

The street was dimly lighted and the lane had slightly up hill to it. When grandmother got out of the cab, she said something to Kimiko in Japanese. She then beet feet up the dimly lighted street.

Yes thank you dear grandmother. There was no one out on the street at this late of night. Kimiko and I are walking I had my arm around her. Stopping in the shadows of the night, I pulling her intimately closer I slowly; so very, very gentle kissing her moist lips. I would have like to make it list longer.

That was the first time I had kissed her. We walked on passing my place. Stopping just in side her gate, in the shadows of the gate it self. We kissed the mother of all kisses A long drawn out gentle kiss. Her lips slightly parted as the fire in our bodies increase, I slowly insert my tongue slightly beyond her lips. Kimiko eyes opened wide then slowing closing ones more in her excepting my tongue.

She then slowly inserted her tongue flicking my tongue with hers. Now that rings my chimes when she kisses me with all the loveshe had in her. Our hearts become one we have to stop. Her grandmother was there in the yard up next to the house. We would have oyher times so we walked on to the house cooling down some.

The house sit back from the gate some 90 yards or so, grandmother was there waiting four us.

The three of us arrived at Kimiko front door together.

I said to grandmother "Thank you, and good night I had a nice time to night, I hope you took pleasure in the theater. Good night and my only happiness fill your home Grandmother."

The old woman bowed and stepped in side the door to give Kimiko and I a minute to say our good nights.

I kissed her good night, turned and walked away.

After I was back out on the street, I said to my self all in all it's been a good night.

Saturday about 7:00 A. M. my old gardener come to my bedroom door he said "some one has come to see you."

I put on my Japanese robe went out to see who was intruding on me I was sleeping in on Saturday.

I was Kimiko's brother; he was a bit older in his mid 20's and married. Coming to the door I said "come in I was about to have coffee, would you join me.

He said "my wife and Kimiko are out in the car." Cutting him off, putting my hand out to the gardener and saying pleas.

The old man was out the door, to the car saying coming in. Jim ask if you like to come in." The three of us sit at the kitchen table in the nook. The cook served coffee and sweet rice cakes. The brother was inviting me to come along on a drive over to Sagamihara to see a shrine. Kimiko smiling at me and nodded in agreement. If I have a half a chance to be with Kimiko. Us go right now! However I just said "It's a nice day for a drive in the country, Yes I would like to come along." The four of us was off to see what we can see. Brother and I was in the front with sister-in-law and Kimiko was in the back.

The sister-in-law can't speak English so Kimiko has to translate so that the way that gose. All she can say is hello and goodby that all she can say.

He brother was telling me all about Japan and how beautiful the country was.

I'm thinking to my self the most beautiful part of Japan is right here in the back sit of this car.

We drove for about a half an hour, when he pulled into a serves station to top up with gas.

Sister-in-law, Kimiko and I got out and walked around to the side of the station. There was a small stream with a waterfall the stream was going through some woods, it was pleasing to the eye.

However I can not keep my eyes off her. Sister-in-law returns to the car. Kimiko and I walked back to the car. Sister-in-law was in the front with her husband. Kimiko and I got in the back; we drove pass a lot of small farms. Five or ten acres how the hell can a farmer make a good of that.

We are holding hands like two school children. We kissed now and then.

When we arrived at Sagamihara brother knew about where the shrine was.

Now parking in Japan can be a all day job. He found a parking lot that was not full, parked and locked the car. Said "see you two back here at 6:00 O'clock."

Him and his wife walked off leaving Kimiko and I their with out an escort. You know what was in this sailor's mind-0-yes.

The fox just got into the chicken house

However Kimiko don't see eye to eye on this most earth shaking moment. We walked to the Buddhist shrine; Kimiko went up and said a prayer. I stayed out side even I'm don't a Buddhist I did not wont to be a martyr After the shrine we walked around and come up on a small park. We sit under a large old tree.

Kimiko was lying back on me as she looked up at me I bent down and kissing her gentle. Smiling up at me arching arms up around my neck, Pulling me down to her. She kiss me on the lips and on the side of the neck then over to the other side of my neck and back to my lips running her tongue deep in to my mouth.

Then it was over she sit up and moved away sitting beside me. Said did you like that? If you did there more, but not here. The time has passed so quickly, Kimiko and I did not get back to the car; it was after 7:00 O clock.

Around 7:15 they come walking to. He asks "do you want to stay for the fireworks, with rockets and firecracker."

The women said yes we would like to stay for the show. The four of us walk back to the park.

Kimiko and I sit on the grass under the big old tree as before.

Kimiko was lying back in my arms we are kissing. The fireworks were going off in the sky, and if she doesn't stop French kissing I'm going to go off just like a rocket in the sky.

I looked over at brother and his wife they were entangling within one another's arms.

After the fireworks in the sky was over. The two couples walking back to the parking lot in peaceful tranquility.

Quietly enter their car and silently slipping away into the shadows of the night.

We are in the back sit of a small little car speeding through the night passing the frame land only the shadows of the houses was all you could see.

We are passionately kissing, I kissed her lips, and her eyes, then her ears, kissing her neck and down to her breast, Running my tongue around her nipples filling my mouth of her breast tongued her belly down to just above her hear.

Kimiko's breath was coming in hot ragged gasps. Pulling my head up to her lips kissing me. Pulling me ever intimately near to her with eager emotion and with a deep down desire. A fire deep with in each of us. Kimiko stopping at just half way. We're hotter than any fire works we had seen that night, in the sky over Sagamihara. Up on our arrival at Kimiko home, her brother pulled the car into the courtyard.

As Kimiko alighted from the she was in front of me as we walked away from the car. I was hopping she did not look back tell I got my man hood down and under control.

I was hoping she would come home with me that night. I need and wanted her that night more than I can say.

But she stopped at her gate. Having her hand in mine I slightly tug her hand so she would come home with me that night.

Kimiko saying "no, not tonight my loved one, not tonight."

I kiss her good night and then she kisses me good night.

I pulling her intimately and passionately in to me with a French kiss knowing she is felling my physically man hood up on her as we kiss once more.

She pulled out of my arms saying "please go, before I say stay." Obeying her urgent request, he said good night.

Walking on home saying to my self "all in all it has been good day; to day." We still waked hand in hand from the bus stop to my gate we would talk sitting out by my front gate. the next week end, the four of us went to the zoo in Tokahama, then other places. We would go to the moves with grandmother as an escort. I got to see that grandmother would watch high and fist moving shows. so that was what we would see. At first Kimiko did not know why I would pick that movie over others. Then when Grandmother would get into the move. We would move to the back row where other young couples were sitting we could kiss and know one would look at you.

One night we are in the back sit of that small little car of Brother kiss her nipples running my tongue over them sliding my hand down into her pants she did not stop me this time play fitfully movement my hand in her. As we come in to the city lights, put her undergarments up and sitting up said "thank GOD we are home you get me needing you, but we don't have that right."

The next day being Sunday I just moped around the house the best part of the day. It was around three in the afternoon I went into have my bath. I'm laying in the hot tub soaking away the day out of my mine. I was thinking about Kimiko what has happen and what was going to happen. Am I doing right by her? I will be going state side before long will never see her any more. At that moment, the bathroom door slide open. Kimiko steps in closed the door behind her. She turns to me and let her kimono drop to the floor.

Stepping down into the water, come over and sit beside me. The tradition rule where sat out side at this time.

We are kissing each other passionately.

With a deep and eager desire we made love their in the bath. After; We are kissing and entangle in each other.

Before one of us drowns we moved into the bedroom.

Kimiko rolled out the bed, we're suffocating each other with kisses, yes it was great.

Right at this tiny moment of time, a time of excellence timing.

I am so high up pn the clouds, if I was to die right at this moment it would take the undertaker two weeks just to get the smile off my face.

The moment of passion has past as the light of day inters the bedroom. Kimiko lay sleeping beside me.

I'm thanking I'm lower than **WHALE SHIT:**

To all of you land lover whale shit is at the bottom of the ocean.

I was the first man she had ever been with, and I'll be going states side before long. I will not be coming back to Japan.

Kimiko 's father was right no man will ever marry her now, she is used goods. I bent over and kissing her a wake, Kimiko smiles up at me and said good morning. That makes it all just a bet better. My hand found her breast as she pulled me down on top of her we made love. Now I'm late I got a taxi cab to the ship.

The time passes to quickly days into weeks and weeks. We are liven as husband and wife out of wedlock.

We are in love; Love is what makes the world go round.

yes; love can make you. Love can break you.

Yes the power of love was up on us. I love this woman so ; I would do anything she wanted me to do.

I know she would give up her life for me, if I was to ask her.

Yes the power of love was up on us.

The good times are giving way to better improved times, with a more desirable time.

I can see the end coming, the day approach.

The young couple with ever increasing speed.

How swiftly the time passes them by. In the last few days that remain.

The Jupiter time to rotate back to San Francisco will be up on the young couple.

Being so much in love in their youth. Time had on place in there lives. Their love is like the cherry blossom of Japan on one can not stop them from budding out. Their love was liken to the flower bud. Who on GODS green earth can, or should even try to stop either.

I knew this time would come. Kimiko' s father also having the foresight knew it would. That was why her father was so inflamed with the two of us. Kimiko don't know we have only 90 more days before the Jupiter sailing date will arrive.

We have only lived as man and wife for only 6 short months.

May day a Japanese holiday with dancing in the streets. That night she and I went up to the park on the top of the hill by our home. Their we can see the rockets go off out over the bay.

When we arrived her family was there. Kimiko parents sat on a park bench, her brother and sister-in-law was up away from the parents.

That night; if looks could kill. I would have been dead. For her father gave me the look of death, as we approached them.

He said something to Kimiko in Japanese that hurt her deeply. After we returned home from the park Kimiko and I was sitting in the kitchen having a coffee before we went to bed. Sitting there hand in hand I'm looking into her eyes. Our two employees had turn in for the night. So we had the place to our selves.

Tell me what your father said to you that hurt you so deeply. He said I was the disgrace on the house of Amato living here with you an not marred he can not go out of the house with being in disgrace. She will be left alone separated from the family and you will never come back to Japan for me. What man would have any thing to do with me after you have use me and then went back to American. What do I do then?

I stood up went around the table getting down on my knees. I ask Ms. Kimiko Amato will you be my wife and marry me. I'll be the best husband I know how to be.

Kimiko said; Yes I will marry you!

On May 15,1953 in a Japanese civil marriage ceremony, Kimiko and Jim, become as one as we enter into HOLY WEDLOCK.

On June 11, 1953 the U. S. S. Jupiter (A V S-8).

Sailed for San Francisco, California.

Before docking at Naval Air Station in Alameda, California. Now my good buddy (the sea lawyer) Gees he said "Jim don't turn in your Japanese marriage license to the navy department. For if you do, you know the Navy will Court Marshal you and that will be the end of your naval career. You know the military laws on Japanese marriages. Here away around this law.

When the ship arrives at Alameda Naval Air Station, You get on the telephone to Kimiko and have her to take a vacation here in San Francisco.

You two can fall in love and get married in Reno.

The Navy is Happy;

You are also Happy.

You have not infringed up on the military law. So ever one is shit happy." Even under full power that's around 15 or 16. The old ship did not arrive in Alameda for seventy four days.

You know that is a lift time for the two youthful lovers. AS Kimiko and Jim are. When I phoned Kimiko the telephone was the old kind. You have to say over; then the other one can talk at then they would say over. It was like that up to around 1960. I would phone her ever other day just to hear her voice. I would ask about her mother. If her farther is mad about us? How are the others doing, and if she needed any thing. I has half out of my min knowing it would be a week more before I can see my love of my life.

Dees and his wife helped find an apartment, and making it livable.

The apartment had a car port, so I don't have to park my baby the 1940 Ford out on the street. Ever one on the ship knew I was waiting for Kimiko to come in at San Francisco air port.

The old man (commanding officer) even ask about when Kimiko was to arrive. He said if he can help you two don't hesitate to ask. If you need time off we can work out some basket leave.

Now all you land lovers; basket leave is what we call it when you need time off. I moped the apartment ever night, and move thing around from here to there from one side of the room to the other side.

To make the time go by quieter, the days was not to bad. But the nights where S. O. B.

The day finale come Kimiko was coming in to San Francisco airport, I went insane with happiness. I do not know how I would have got to and from the airport.

With out Dees and his wife helping out driving me. I would been going hundred miles an hour down the freeway if I had been driving.

Dees said he was like that when he was going to Texas to get married.

Like the man said "Love can make you do what ever you have to do, all just for a good woman."

That afternoon Kimiko' s plane arrived at San Francisco air port (S. F. O.).

I was there by the security gate but when I seen her step off the plane I run to her we are the only two people in the world. My arms around her kissing as if it had been ten years not just under a hundred days. We retrieved her bags and walked out to the car. We drive in to the city. I knew she would like to see San Francisco. We are in the back sit of Dees car kissing we did not see the city. We crossed over the bay bridge into Oakland then the 23 street bridge into the city of Alameda and on to our small apartment I had rented for us.

Dees put the bags inside and said later my man. We walked to the front door where I picked up Kimiko and stepping in side and closing the door. I sit her down so she can see the apartment.

I removed my clothes, and helping her out of her dress. We are kissing. I'm kissing her lovely beautiful breast. Flicking her nipples with my tongue. She saying "US** US."

O' honey ** I'm going to** yes I'm going to; O' yes; after. We are laying in each other's arms.

I moved us to the bed and laying her down. She is saying "Jim you don't know how good you feel to me." After the next time around we are in bed.

She said "it's been a long time and I like all you do to me you make me so hot I can not stop my self."

Saying "Honey I thank you destroyed my insides. I thank you about killed me. You are bigger than I remembered. We stop now all right. Later that afternoon we are about to make love, I went in to the bathroom gat a bath cloth and putting it around my man hood so I would not destroy her insides. This worked all right that night.

The first weekend I had stand by duty. I can go home however I have to be on the ship with in a half hour. So the next weekend we went to Reno, Nevada. We lived in Alameda, California. Jim; was still station on the Jupiter at Naval Air Station Alameda. It was just a short drive from our place to the ship. Then the Jupiter went up to Vallejo, California at the Mare Naval shipyard in to dry-dock now that is one more hour driving time coming home at night.

But none of that mattered it's unimportant.

We are in love and living in Alameda, California.

If we where in the streets we would still be in love. Love makes the world go round. Love can make you sleep out in the cold rain.

I love this woman so; I would do anything for her. she is my woman; she is my wife; she is my life; and we are in love. Fortunately we have a place to call home.

We don't have to live on the streets.

This one day I was going about my duties on board the ship there was a (I. S. P.) phone call from the office they ask me to come up to the duty office so I did.

Happy Days are here, My orders come in for me to report to Naval Air Station, at Corpus Christi, Texas.

I think GOD, no more ship, I'm a sailor that don't like sea duty!

A new way of life with my wife. (**No More Fucking Ships**)

I have my cherry 1940 Ford three window coupe. Kimiko and three suitcases ; one sea bag ; and two small boxes. One car load of love. As it turned out the old Ford was not as much in love as Kimiko and I!

It stopped running in southern California.

We check into a motel for the night.

Now I don't know what, but what ever it was, the coastal breeze or just knowing I had got off that ship. I just don't know but what ever it was I can not get no satisfaction. We made love all night and the next day, and the day after that. We made love over and over for two days and nights I still have a deep desired for more of Kimiko' s loving. We went out to eat after that I looked at the car to have it repaired. Now that is what I would call ; honeymoon number two.

I had the generator replaced and the battery charged. We lift for Kansas the next day. We stopped off to see my brother just out side of Taos, New Mexico. That's over by the Rio Grande.

We went horse back ridding. Kimiko said "I can not ride a horse I have never been near a horse before!

Will you know we all had to tell her "that it would be all right it is the first time the horse has been rode. So you two can start off a new." She watched Bob and me get on and off our horses two or three times. She got up on her horse and off we went.

The next day we said our good by to Bob and his wife. We drove over to see mother and father the farm is 15 miles north west out of Caldwell, Kansas. Caldwell is small around 800 hundred is all. When we pulled up the drive way. I can see the old farm, at this time of the afternoon Dad will be milking the cows Mom will be in the house cooking or out helping Dad. I stop the car and we got out Mom seen it was my car come out of the house. Saying J.D. your home! and this is Kimiko I'm so happy to see you two. J. D. when are you going to get a car that you can drive to Corpus Christi in, and know you are going to get there all in one piece

I went out to see Dad and help out if I can.

the next day Dad said he had to check the east side chack to see if they had water.

I said Dad let Kimiko and me check it.

Good O. K. He need to some work around here.

I had Kimiko to drive the feeder truck she did good. We stopped at the gate I would get out and open the gate and she would drive through and stop for me. she was driving good by the time we departed for my sisters place out side of Dallas we were there only one night she had to work the next day. So we went on to Corpus Christi.

We arrived nine days before I had to check in at the Naval Air Station. We drove out to see where I would be working.(A M D)

We rented a small apartment in the city to wait for the navy housing. We moved in three suitcases one sea bag and two small boxes.

In six months we moved to a bigger apartment a cross the street it took half a day.

Six months later we moved into a two bed room house next door, it took all weekend.

One year later we moved into the old navy housing, The navy sent three men and a truck to move.

Two years more we moved into the new naval housing had to use a moving van.

Two and a half years later we moved to Japan. We are 2'000 pounds over, that I had to pay for.

Four years we moved to the states we sold some of the larger size items we where 7,600 pounds over. The navy would move 20,000 and a car. When we moved up here to Oregon I had to pay for it all. Andrew moved 20,000 pounds, and He took some of the bigger items in the F350 Ford. So no more moving, we don't need what ever it is. Oregon is our last move.

Going back to the time I reported into VT 27 at Naval Air Station Corpus Christi, Texas for duty at that time I did not know it would be for so long of duty not quite 10 years.

In that ten years Kimiko become an American citizen with a new American name it's Kim.

We had an addition to the family, Lyn, JR. and Andrew the baby of the family. I recall how I loved there mother of my three children.

Kim's mother was in hospital. I did not have the finances to send her to Japan to see her mother. I obtain an off duty employment, driving a 8,000 gallon gasoline truck on my days off. I would drive 32 hours on the week end. Friday night to Monday and 20 hours or more in the week days. From Flour Bluff to Viola station about 80 miles round trip. One hour to load and a half an hour to unload. Some times I would drive up to San Antonio

As it happen the trucking company paid me more than the navy.

I had over $3,000..oo in wages from Skerlock Oil Company.

Kim had put in for and received her American passport, but her Japanese Visa the authorization to enter Japan had not arrived as of yet, more delays. Kim phoned her father, he had good news he said "your mother is out of hospital and doing good. She is out side right now I will call her." They talked for some time, the phone bill was going to be out of this world. The navy come through after all the years in Texas. I received my orders. Marine Core Air Station M. C. A. S. (N. A. S. U.) Iwakuni Japan for three year with family. I had 90 days of schooling to get back up to speed after 10 years in VT-27 I needed the school.

Come moving day Kim had to divide the move in to three, one going to the 90 days schooling, one going to Japan so we would have what we needed when we would be looking for a house, the big one.

A sailor offered to pay more then my 40 Ford would ever be worth. I sold it to the sailor.

We got a new 1969 Ford for $2,800.00 that was new off of the show room floor, and had money lift over from my 1940 Ford.

On the way to California, we stopped in west Texas it was away out from any place seeing a restaurant so I pulled in to the parking lot. Their was a sign, No Mexicans.

I went in side and ask the red neck "how about Japanese?" I was going to kick some ass over that sign. But the red neck said 'O' that sign that just to keep the Mexicans from the other side of the border out. The border patrol is in here all the time that is why the sign the border patrol has said the next time they see a south of the border Mexican in here they was going to close me down.

I went to school and it helped me out a lot. After the school was over we sit around for a week and no order to move on to Japan. The personal office ask me if I'd like to go to Japan on a ocean liner the S, S. Grover Cleveland of the Presidential lines. It stopped at L.A. and the Islands and on to Japan. I said I have to talk it over with the family. He gave me a flyer about the ship.

That night I ask Kim and the child if they would like that. The child all said yes, can we go on the ship? Kim ask can we fly over? Yes we can go however you would like to go. The child all said come on Mom us go on the Ship! After they keep it up she said yes we will go by ship. The next day I said to the personal officer Yes the family would like to go on the S. S. Grover Cleveland of the Presidential Lines. Kim was all right from San Francisco to L. A. but when we departed L. A. Kim got sea sick and was sick all the way to Japan. The child and I had a ball more food than you can eat. I would go up the main dick and have coffee with the others that had been in Japan. Each day we be one hour a head so we would be up at 4:30 or 5:00 in the A. M. to have coffee and shoot the shit. 24 hours room service.

When the taxi stopped at the end of the road. Kim and our family were all standing there at the side of the street. The old house we first made love in the old tree by the street light where we first kissed. with more and more thing. My eyes where full of tears. As we walked on up the block when we come to our old gate. Kim said to the children this was you daddies house when we got married, the house we made into a home. We walking on to Kim's parents house. Her gate had been replaced by a newer one. The older one was the one Jim remembers Where they had kiss go night and some time hello.

as we come to it. The gate open by it's self walking on to the house it closed by it's self. I'm keeping the children back to let Kim would be the first to say her greeting to her family.

All of her family come rushing out to greet us. there was Brother and his wife, Her mother and grandmother was slower to come out but their she was. My father-in-law with tears of happiness in his greeting. The man ten years ago. This old man would of like to have killed me for taking there first girl child away to America.

The first day at Kim parents home the children come running out to the garden where Kim, her father and I was sitting. The three of them said "Mommy; Grandma's food is Au-Keee."

Grandpa saying you have three American children that don't like Japanese food. You will have to cook for your family.

Kim was in the house doing the cooking for the children when I come in from the garden.

It may have been the smoke from the charcoal or the longing for home. Kim had tears in her eyes.

I ask what is it, as I'm kisses away the tears.

She answered "It my parents, they look so old." The following day I got my brother-in-law and wife off to one side out away from the house.

I said "Brother-in-law you tell your wife how much I'm in your and her debt. If we had not taken the drive to Sagamihara to see shrine and the fire works. I thank you." He was speaking to his wife in Japanese when Kim up to join us. Kim said "Yes dear brother and sister we thank the two of you." Then Kim putting her arm around my neck pulling me down to her. Kiss me just a bet to long.

At that time her brother said to his wife "Why don't you ever kiss me like that?" Bowing her head in the Japanese custom putting her hand on his four arm as all four of us walked back to the house.

Brother said he was glad you two got married he was running out of zoos to go to. The family and I arrived at Iwakuni five days before I was to report in to N. A. S. U. the three years of duty that turn out to be four years.

Kim got us a old house off base, It hundred percent Japanese. The children did not know what to think about it. It was all new to them, there mother speaking Japanese, the cars driving on the other side of the street. After they got in to the school and they would walk to school all new children to them. Had to show there Navy I. D. 's to go through the gate going on and off the base. In three months they had made this way of life work for them. The house was heated by three space heaters using coal/oil. The serves station Japanese he can not speck English and I no Japanese.

So it would take a half hour to get it through to him what I wonted.

I got some Arigato Business cards printed up after that I would go in to order more coal/oil him and his truck would bet me home so that worked out all right. After a year and a half the housing office phone me said they had a house on base if I

45

would like to look it over come and get the key. As I come into the housing office, their was a marine officer in the office just raising hell about he would do this and that if the house officer did not get him a house to day.

The Naval housing officer eye to eye to me. Saying "If you just have to have a house to day you can take this house I was going to issue officially to this naval officer."

The Jar/Head talking his shit, signed the papers with out looking at the house. The housing officer issued him two keys.

After the jar/head had departed. The housing officer said "that shit head, Jim you have been on the list for will over a year now. Two more days don't make that much difference.

Here the keys to the house I was going put him into, drive past look it over and see if you like it or not. So I drove by to look it over it was in the senior officers housing.

I went back to the housing office, I said "yes I would like to have it but that it's senior officers housing. I'm to low on the totem/pole to move in to that house."

He said "do you like it?" "Hell yes I like it."

"It is yours then, I have had it with those *^&%$#@ jar/headed marines." I'll sign for it right now.

I said "come on over to the club I owe you one."

We moved on the base the next week it was like moving back to the states. The house was so close I would walk to work. The children's school was just down the street no roads to cross. We had room for her parents to come to see us. It was a suite for the house keeper it was down on the main floor. We would go in to town maybe once a week the service station where I go the coal/oil get a car wash but the Ford would not go through The Japanese women working the carwash don't wont to see that car to show up, for they would have to wash it by hand. So I would geve each one that wash on the car 100 yen ($.35) each after three or four times like that. When I pulled in to have a carwash the women would wave to come to there work station. We are about to come to the time to go state side. So Kim and I drove up to the Ford place in Hiasemi The man that was going to buy the car keep looking at the license tags and saying some thing In Japanese and Kim was in having tee. The sale/man come in and come over to us. I ask what is he saying about the license tags the sale/man said he is going to have to pay 89% tax 1,325,600 yen tax. he paid me $4,500= 1,642,500 yen That was for a three year car. That went I got it I paid $2,800 new off the show room floor.

He was paying 2,968,100 yen or $8,460 when in San Francisco You can get a new Ford for around $ 3,300 t0 $3,500 but when we got back the new Ford was over $8,000

On July 21 1973 we departed Nasu and I retired from the Navy. After 23 years in the Navy.

I opened up my own business at 101 Appian Way in Union City, California I did not renew the lease.

After I moved on from that to only working when I like to.

Chapter Two

From Kimiko

The young people of Japan are a blend of east and west. They follow many traditional customs of old Japanese way of life. But they also enjoy the western way of life.

Kimiko Amato was no exception.

Where I live it has a big court yard when you come through the gate the crematorium was on the right side of the drive way. Tacking up just under 1/5 of the lot. Father was in the funeral business. You see my father is the town undertaker. Fifty yards pass the crematorium over on the other side of the road over to the left side of the court yard my house sat. The court yard was a big one over four hector (1 hectare = 2.47 acres) that is 9.88 acres.

At the age of 20 years old, I remember my school days. All of the women I went to school with are all married and some even have children. Heir I am, I don't even have a man caller to call on me.

I will never get married. Here I'm going on to 21 and don't have any one to even call on me. All I ever do is go to the market for mother, and then right back home. I don't ever go out with old high school friends. I just know I'm going to be an old maid spinster a lone isolated from family and friends.

My Brother name is Brother he was married at my age and they are so happy with each other.

All I ever do is stay home and sometimes go out with brother and my sister-in-law to a show then back home.

Then one day on the way to the market as I stepped out of the gate turned and closed the gate. I was on my road to do the daily shopping.

Closed the gate and turning to go. I seen at the other end of the block three men in shining white garments with golden medals that was awarded for merit.

They shined in the sun with a blinding bright light of the sun. I put up my hand to block the sun. So I can see these shining Samurai with their swords of gold and silver as they come my way.

The three turned and vanishes they just disappeared off the street into a gate. I was one house away when they disappeared in to the gate.

I'm thinking to myself, my what handsome men. Maybe if I look in the gate way where they had disappeared I can see them.

My mind leaping out of control, fantasizing in my daydream about A Samurai warrior that would take me away from my uneventful day to day existences that I am in now.

But by the time I arrived at the gate they were out of sight.

My normal mental condition once was intact.

I went on to the market, as I returned I looked in the gate where the three silver and golden Samurai had vanishes. All I seen was some men with their shirts off.

I like the looks of the small one with black hair even if he was not a shining golden Samurai.

That afternoon I told my sister-in-law Locus, about what I had seen, Locus said "You are nuts, you say you seen three golden Samurai, with swords of gold and silver." I have to go to the market with you next time. So I can see what kind of tea you are having at the market that makes her see the Samurai.

The next day Locus and I went to the market place as we passed the house of the Samurai, there was no one about.

We went on to the market, on the way home we seen a old man working in the garden.

Locus said "How do you do sir. Who were the men I seen coming into your home the other day."

The gardener said "You are talking about the three men who has rented this house. My wife and I work for the three American sailors off a ship in the bay."

Locus and I said good day sir.

We walk on so the old man can't hear us Locus said to me as we walked on home "Three Samurai? You see three American Sailors and you think you seen three Samurai, you are out of your tree! That is what you are."

Two weeks had past I seen the Americans going and coming to their house. The small sailor smiles at me each time he sees me. There is a Tall one I think he is handsome but to tall. The other one is big and tall and fat.

The one that smiles at me all the time, he is smaller than the other two.

One day the old woman that cooks for the three American come running to my house. She was saying "Would you come and translate from English to Japanese to speak to the Americans sailors for me."

I went with the cook as we arived the old cook woman said "The Americans would like to go to the Ginza in Yokohama."

I'm thinking to myself if the Americans would like for me to show the way that would be nice. I can use my school English and just maybe they will pay me to translate for them.

The small one with the black hair did the taking for the three of them. "Hello my name is Kimiko and as I understand it you are in need of someone to translate for you that if my information is correct."

The smaller one said "Yes we need someone to teach us what buss and what train to take to Yokohama."

"I would be most happy to show you. However in Japan you know an unmarried young woman needs to have an escort."

He said "Who can you get to be an escort for us?"

I replied "I'll go and see if my married aunt would like to go."

As I walk back to my house, I was thinking to myself the smaller American sailor is nice and somewhat handsome.

I ask one of my aunt's if she would like to go with us to Yokohama She said "yes". My other aunt and my grandmother all wanted to go with us. We went back to the three sailors house, I ask if the two aunt's and grandmother could go.

We got the bus to the train station I showed Jim how to see where the bus was going. I don't know if he could read the sign on the bus or not but he would say that one is the one going to the house and that one I don't know where it is going. When we arrived at the Ginza. My aunt's and my grandmother were like three young children. Laughing and happy going here and their.

The tall American the one by the name of Dees went into the nightclub and the tall fat one walked alone. The nice one with the smile walk with grandmother and I. His name is Jim.

Jim ask through me if my grandmother and my aunt's would like some food, I had to translate between grandmother and Jim. We eat at a nice restaurant.

Grandmother said to me in Japanese so Jim would not understand.

"This American has money, not because he spent so much yen here in the Ginza. But look at his shut and his shoes and the way he walks, he knows what is going on around him all the time. Just look at them other two, one is a drunken I don't know what. The other one is a big fat pig." He has spent 5 or 6,000 yen here today that around $16.50 that is what he would spend in America if he went out by himself. Jim would talk to my aunt's or to my grandmother and I would translate for them. Jim would say things just to make them laugh, we all had a good time.

Jim went into the nightclub and got the tall one by the name of Dees. On the train I showed Jim the train sign to go to Yokohama and back home. I knew he did not know what the sign said. I just hopped he could find his way. We went to the bus stop and when our bus come Jim said this is our bus, and he was right. When we got off the bus Jim put a note in my hand, I can't wait tell I'm in my room with the door closed to see what his note had to say. My heart began to beat rapidly and I was deeply moved about it all.

My palms of my hands where sweating, as I open my hand to see what Jim's note said.

It was just a 10,000 yen bill ($27.40) in American. That was a good tip back in those days. However I was hopping he had wrote a nice note.

After that the tall one moved back to the ship. In a week or so the other one moved back to the ship. I did not see them anymore.

Latter Jim told me they moved back to the ship.

I did see more of Jim, He did not know I would wait at the bus stop to see him. He would walk with me to his home at the gate.

We would sit at his gate and talk. He asked me if I would like a cup of coffee, saying the cook had it on the table when he come home at night. I had to say no, an unmarred women can never enter a unmarred man house without an escort and then after knowing him for a long time and the escort said it was all right and with others in the house. So we said good night at his gate and he would go in and I would go on home. I would daydream how it would be if some night he'd take me into his arms and kiss away all the loneliness I have in side of me. Sometimes when we sit beside his gate and talked. I would daydream about us, fantasy my desires, fulfilling my endless desire To a point which my loneliness no longer existed.

This sailor was nice not like my friends say. They work down town and they told me about the American sailor, they are all bad men.

One afternoon I made Jim some rice cakes and we sit at his gate and talked. for some time He had the cook to bring us out coffee and ask me if coffee was all right or would I like tea. We sit out in front of his house and had coffee and rice cake.

My heart jumped a beat when his hand brushed my hand.

I'm uncomfortable warm, as I look into his sympathetic eyes his mouth looked inviting.

What would he do if I was to kiss them lips affectionately?

As we sit their side by side on that old stone wall.

I ask myself if these stones could talk what would they say?

What of others that sit here 10, 12, or one hundred years ago

Maybe a Japanese sailor and his love one before he went off to war and never returned. Who knows the identity of the lovers that was here before us. Was others sit here before Jim and I. What has happen to them did they drift apart and go they own ways.

Maybe a hundred years ago, two lovers here at this gate. Sit on the new stone wall. Was the marks made by her as she prayed rubbing the stones with her hands year after year as she prayed. For the love of her life that never come back. The friction over the years had put the marks in the stones. Tell she become old and one day she never return to pray. When they laid her in the ground did she see her love one that she had prayed for. So long ago?

Jim black hair was cut short. I would like to feel his hair to see if it's as soft as it looks. My heart beats faster when he moved near me, His arm touching my breast. As he moves the basket back from the edge of the stone wall, so it would not fall off the stone wall.

He asked once more if I would like some tea or a glass of water. The old cook can serve tea, coffee, beer, or as soft drank.

I said "No, thank you."

After a time I said well maybe just a small glass of water.

Just a minute. He came out of the kitchen door with a tall glass of water in one hand, and his coffee in the other. He handing me the glass of water and he sit back on the stones with his coffee in hand he raised the cup to his lips and allowing the hot coffee to inter that most enticing mouth.

He place a brooch into my hand saying it was from the Republic of the Philippines.

As we sit at his gate talking that evening. Jim said he was the state of Kansas.

Was Kansas in the United States of America, I'm thinking. I never heard of a state by the name of Kansas. When I got home I took out my old school book with a map of the United States of America and read about his home. So he would think I knew.

Kansas is in the middle of the United States of America.

To the south side is Oklahoma,

On the east side is Missouri,

On the north side is Nebraska and

On the west side is Colorado.

The biggest city is Wichita named after the Wichita Indians of America.

My father is so mad at me!

Someone told him I like that American sailor that lives down the street. That ever afternoon we walk from the bus stop to his house and sit outside his gate on the old stone wall and talk in English.

Bowing my head on the floor in submission I answered his question. "Yes Father!"

"I do walk with the American his name is Jim. Father we just talk in English is all."

Father said "I've told you over and over not to have anything to do with any of the foreigners that has come to Japan."

Farther said "all sailors are the same, no good. Your American sailor will be like all the other sailors. When he leaves Japan he will never return. He will never come back, he has a home in the United States of America. He will disgrace the woman and her family and never even look back. After he is through with you he will cast you a side and go on to the next port of call!"

"After that no Japanese man that is a man would never marry with you!"

I said "but father what is so bad about him and I talk outside his house on the side of the street?" father said you are a woman now not my small child. You go and do what you would like.

That next week end Father and Jim's gardener had just a little alcoholic beverages especially to excess, talking there drunk talk.

Jim come out of his house and walked over to where they sat.

Jim saying to my father "Sir your daughter will be safe with me, I'm a gentleman.

I have nothing but honorable intention. I will not mention the young lady's name, when I'm with you drunkards. A good mannered gentleman just doesn't! I will never embrace or disgrace your daughter in any way or will I ever disgrace the name of the Amato house."

After that day father was just a little angry at Jim.

This one afternoon my family and I were going to a small park at the top of a hill near my house, we would just walk up to it. Me and the family was going up to the park just for time with each other for the family to be a family at the closing of the day. One can look out over the water and see the sun go down it was a nice place to spend time at the end of the day.

As father and mother was passing Jim's gate. Jim come out of his gate.

Father said in Japanese "if your young man would like to come with us, he is welcome."

Closing the gate and turning he sew me. I said "we are going to the hill top park. Would you like to come with us, you are welcome."

Jim said no your father would not approve of me going with your family.

But father just now ask if you would like it is all right. If I ask you to come with the family.

Jim had on his Japanese happy coat, the style a man would use around the neighborhood.

I said "you look handsome in your happy coat of blue and white.

Jim said and you are looking beautiful this evening. We walk side by side with mother and father a head of us.

At the hilltop park one can look down in to the bay and can see the ships there in the bay. I ask "Jim witch one of the ship are you on" He said the one with the big eight on its side.

My father sat there strict in the Japanese traditional style.

Father holding out his hand for Jim to come and sit with him.

Father said "you may call on my house if you would care to, and you may call on Kimiko any time with her consent."

I was so happy that was father's way of saying Jim can come courting me. To see each other with an escort any time we did not have to ask father each time we go out.

The next day mother said "You will invite your American, this Sunday to come for tea. You will serve and carry out your duties to your guest within the tea ceremony in the tradition of the Japanese style."

Bowing my head to the floor in submission. Saying "yes mother but what about daddy?" Can I see Jim any time if he comes over on Sunday for tea?"

Mother said we will see. She ask "what is your Americans name"?

I said his name is Jim from the house of McLogue. He is from the land of Kansas in the United States of America.

Mother said that a long way from Japan.

Your father knows when he goes back to his America your hart will go with him. You will pine away year after year and he will never come back to you or even to Japan. Of all the young men of Japan why do you have to fall in love with an American?

It has been over five days from the time father said it was all right for Jim to call on me. He has not called one time.

We walk from the bus stop to his gate and we talk now it is hours we are at his front gate sitting on them old stones wall.

I can't ask him to come and see me at my home. That would not be lady like or proper.

On Sunday mid afternoon Jim arrived at my house. When he arrived at the front door he said good afternoon to my father, and a small bow bending just his head to mother and one to grandmother he would not come in the house tell after my father ask him in. Father ask him to come into my humble home we are happy that you could come this afternoon

Jim was a perfect gust. He removed his shoes just inside the anteroom. I placed the white house shoes on his feet. Mother and father sit at the back of the room.

I was so nervous I can't keep my hand from shaking. I can't put the hot water into the cup without unintentionally spilling it.

I was thinking Jim you are driving me out of my mind, my face was flashed.

My hands are shaking and my knees are weak.

I hand no strength if I would have to stand at this time, I don't think I could.

After the tea ceremony was over father and mother bowed and left the room.

Latter we went in to the garden strolling leisurely, and talking. Holding hands and passing the time away.

My heart was about to jump out of my breast, when Jim ask me if I would like to go to the Kubuki theater in Yokohama next Friday.

I said "Yes I would love to go with you to Yokohama, With grandmother as an escort." After I replied so quickly. Did

I do the right thing? May be he will think I'm too eager, I'm Japanese, I am to be a lady of mystery. Not a wide eyed school girl. Damn I hope he did not notice. If he did he would not say.

I have never toll Jim even this up to this day, but I never did like Kubuki.

Jim come to escort grandmother and I to the theater in Yokohama. He had on a navy blue suit, his eyes dance over me and I can feel the warmth of my blood pounding inside of my body.

The pressure increase shivers of exquisite pleasure rippled through my body.

He ask about the family and saying hello to my father and bowing his head to mother.

The cab was inside the court yard.

Jim put out his arm for me to take. I looked at grandmother she nodded her head down and back up. We made eye contact she gave me a sympathetic wink. I tuck Jim arm as we stepped out of the house, as we walk to the cab.

Jim and I sit in the back of the cab and grandmother sit up by the driver. After the theater we stop and had a late dinner.

We are back home the taxi driver ask if he could turn around if he drove us on up to the house. Grandmother said this is all right.

Grandmother said in Japanese "I have to go to the bathroom." She went on up the hill to the house. Leaving us at the taxi.

Jim and I were walking slowly up the side of the street my hand in Jim's.

In the shadow under the tree where the tree was blocking the street lamp.

To hide my confusion I forced my self to look into Jim's eyes. The pressure increased. Jim's chest was crushing my breasts. A low groan comes from my parted lips.

"You're so beautiful" He whispered softly in my ear. That was when we stopped in the shadows. He putting his arms around me. Smiling wickedly, showing pleasure, he stopped and taking my mouth. While his hands played havoc with my senses.

We kissed our first kiss; his soft touch delicate expressing the tenderness of his lips on mine, our first kiss.

We are holding each other with tenderness.

I kissed him with all I had in me.

I can smell his male essence.

Smelling the outdoors, The smell of wood/smoke. The pine trees.

The heat still radiate between Jim and I. I can feel his hot body heat, his manhood next to me.

I pulled away so I could keep myself in completely control as I was not in control, with me in his arms.

We walked on to my gate stepping in side. I'm saying to myself do I let him kiss me once more?

My heart was going so fast the blood was making me warm all over. Jim has needs and they are grate but I can't help him.

I do hope he under stands.

In the shadow of the gate it's self, Jim pulling me into his arms we kiss a long and gentle kiss as if I was a soft as a delicate flower. It left me weak in the knees.

More kissing like that and I would go home with him. Shiver of pleasure run through my body.

He kissed me with his tongue French kissing me. One of my old class mates was telling us about it. I said I would never do that! But I just Love for Jim to kiss me that way. He can make me longing for more of his kisses.

I am in love with an American. I know my father is right he will never return to me or to Japan.

Grandmother was waiting for us next to the house. The three of us walked to the door to/gather

Jim said to grandmother "goodnight Ms. Amato, I hope you had a good time to night." I had to tell grandmother what he said.

Grandmother bowing and stepping just inside the door way. Out of the way, so Jim and I could say our good nights.

We kissed a small and short kiss good night.

He then turned and walked swiftly a way.

Grandmother said after Jim had gone. "your American sailor boy is a nice man, I like him. I don't understand him but I like him."

The next day was Saturday my brother and his wife Locus where going to Sagamihari.

I ask if I can come along. They said yes. I ask can Jim go also. Would you invite him to come with us.

Borther stopped the car at Jim's house Locus my sister-in-law and I stayed in the auto. Brother went inside to get Jim.

In about twenty minutes Jim's old gardener come out to the auto where Locus and I are waiting.

The old man said "come in please, Sir. James said for me to ask you in. Please come into my masters humble home please." Locus and I went in brother and Jim where in the kitchen having coffee.

Jim's cook served us coffee and rice cakes. After we had our coffee. Locus and I looked at the hallways and the big room was open we could see in side. It was so big for just one man. Locus and I went out to the auto, as Jim was getting ready.

Locus said "Jim must be financially well off back in his Kansas in the States the place he is from, One man in that big house and with two workers. Maybe he is looking for a wife so she can have a large number of babies and filling the big house with children maybe eight or nine or more."

I did not answer her question. I thought to myself that will be my problem.

Locus and I sit in the back of the Auto. I knew father can see us.

So men in the front and women in the back of the Auto. Out of the city Brother stopped for petrol. Locus, Jim and I walk around to the side of the station to look at the trees and the water coming over the falls. It was nice to look at and Jim was there next to me. Locus walked on back to the Auto. Jim and I talk some before returning to the small blue auto it need to be panted but it run so that was all that was needed.

Locus was up front with her husband, Jim and I got into the back.

I would of like for Jim to show some affection; kiss me Just once.

Maybe Jim don't share my feelings.

We went through the country side, Jim put my hand in to his as if we are two school kids.

As we talked about how small the farms are and none of them had a barn or any other farm buildings.

I don't know what he was talking about. The only farms I had ever seen are just the small Japanese farms were all. Jim said his father farms 260 hectares by his self. (640acres).

Jim putting his other hand on the inter side of my upper leg. Rubbing it up and down as he turn to me and kiss me on the lips as I responded to his kiss. Taking his hand off my leg. He had his hand on my breast I slowly removed it.

As we drove on he put his arm around me and kissing once more his fingers playing with my blouse putting his hand under the loose garment touching my skin moving his fingers slowly up and down my bare skin. I moved nearer to him looking up at him he kiss my lips gentle and slowly, as he put his hand on my breast. I pulled his down away from my breast but, I did enjoy the way his fingers worked the nipples. But I had to stop him, my brother and his wife was in the front of the auto. We kiss more, I could feel his manhood rubbing on my body. I put my hand on it, as he bent his head down his lips touching my ear.

A long low moan escaped through my lips.

His lips trailing from my forehead down to the tip of my nose. Before kissing my waiting mouth.

The pressure increased down deep inside my body, as his tongue darted into my mouth.

Back and forth out tongues dueled. A tantalizing male scent clung on Jim's skin and that made me light headed.

Jim lifted his head to look me in the eyes. His hand found away up my back before advancing on to my breasts, I'm already heavy with wont.

I was not wearing a bra having no need of one cupping one of my breast his thumb drew circles around my nipple. When his mouth closed over the other one his tongue flicking my nipple. A slow drawn out moan coming from deep in my throat.

Jim kissing me with his tongue in my mouth I suck it in deep.

I have heard about this kind of kissing and I did not think I would like it.

Jim was the first to ever kiss me with his tongue and, I like it. I hop that don't make me a loose woman. But I like for Jim to kiss me with his tongue.

We arrived at Saganihara my brother parked in an open parking lot locked the auto and said we will see you two back here at 6:00 o'clock. Back here at the auto at 6 all right? Brother and his wife walked off. Jim and I where their with out a escort. Jim pulling me in to his arms to kiss me right there on the sidewalk. Like a street hooker. I said NO not here on the side of the street.

Pulling my self out of his arms. I was blushing and so embraces, just not here!

We walked over to the big old Buddhist Temple. Jim did not go in with me. I said a prayer, that Jim would marry me and we can live in his Kansas.

After the Temple we walked around sight seeing we come to a park and sit down under a big old tree. We are talking and I was laying back against Jim, him have his arms around me his arms in gulping me.

Looking up at the sky with the white puffy clouds floating in that big blue beautiful sky.

Jim makes me blush when he bent down kissing me so gently slowly touching my lips with his.

"Where did the time go?"

It was past time to go back to the auto. When we did arrived back at the auto. Locus and my brother had not returned.

Jim and I walking with our arms around each other, walked in back of a truck in the back of the parking lot and kiss some more.

Locus and brother returned to the parking lot. Brother ask "shell we stay for the fireworks?"

I said "yes us stay."

The four of us walked back over to the park. Jim and I sit under the big tree as before on the grass. Brother and Locus way over by their selves. The shadow are slowly falling over the park engulfing the young lovers. As the fireworks where going off in the sky, they where going off in my heart as I was hopelessly dissolve into my Jim's arms. As he gently kisses my wonting lips.

After the fireworks where over in the sky that night. My heart was still on fire. I'm in Jim's arms. I'm the most hopeless and happiest woman in all of Japan that night.

My heart was rushing faster than before. Jim and I was in the back sit his arms around me. He is suffocating me with his kisses. Slowly he kiss my lips and then he kisses me on my eyes, my neck and when he kiss my breast.

I was thinking; ho GOD, give me the will power to stop him before it's too late and I let him go all the way!

How I wonted Jim. For my needs are like any other 20 year old woman in my serious state of mind. GOD knows I won't to submit to him, but I knew down deep in my heart it was wrong.

But when he is kissing me I don't know right from wrong, up from down. He is kissing my breast running his tongue around my nipples going first to one and then the other using his fingers to play with the nipple he don't have his tongue flickering. I'm so in need of him but I can't let him. We are not marred! I have no right to have sex with him it is so wrong for me to even be thinking of having sex.

I can't; It is so wrong!

Thank GOD we are in the city now it won't be long before we are home. I pushed Jim away from me saying we are about home. Jim stopped kissing my nipples and sit up, removing his hand from my under pants. I pulled my garment down as we drove in the gate at my place.

I walked out to the gate with Jim we kissed some more there at the gate. He lightly tugging at my hand he ask me to come home with him.

I said "no my love not to night." We kissed once more and Jim departed.

I did not sleep at all that night all I can think of is my Jim. The next day was Sunday.

I said to Locus "where is Jim? What can he be doing? I most be going crazy. It is going to be afternoon he has not come to see me. Locus am I crazy to be like this?"

Locus said "I'll go see the cook at Jim's house. I will ask her if I left my sunglasses there the other day."

At the same time I can ask about your Jim. That you are so crazy about."

When Locus returned she said he was about to go in to the hot bath tub.

I ask "Locus what am I to do?"

Locus said Kimiko go to him and sleep with him if he loves you he will marry you and if he don't he won't."

I'm asking "how do I look? Is my kimono all right or what about this other one?"

Locus saying "You look nice, very nice in deed." When I inter into Jim's house.

I come into his home for ever as I can't never return to my home after this.

If Jim rejects me and drives me from his home. Or what if he use me and then drive me out. I'll have to kill myself in disgrace.

I went to the bathroom door where Jim is in the hot tub.

Hesitating at the door. If I return home now on one will know what I'm about to do.

I put my hand on the door once more hesitated thinking what if he don't love me and puts me out. Or he used me and then puts me out!

GOD forgave me! I have to go to the man I love with all my love I will gave all to him.

I open the door and step into the bathroom closing the door after me.

Jim was in the hot tub he looked up at me.

As I step in and removed my Kimono dropping it to the floor.

I'm stepping into the water as a girl and into woman hood in Jim's arms.

He was so gentle let me take my time. I don't know what I wonted not the pain but I did wont Jim inside of me. He was so gentle with me and I loved him for it.

I slept in my man's arms that night.

Monday Jim went to work on the ship for a half a day. When he come home at noon we had some after noon delight.

We did not leave the house one time in them two weeks.

Then he return to his daily duties on the ship. He would leave the house at 5:30 and come walking up the hill at 5:30 I'm at the door ever night to welcome him home. I would remove his shoes asking about his job. If he won't a hot bath, food, water or me!

I was so happy even if we are not married. I ask Jim if I can have some of my girlfriends over some afternoon. As I would like to show them our home. I have been in their homes and seen their children and their men.

He said yes that would be good we can get to know my friends we can have a party. How about this Saturday afternoon ?

'O' no not this Saturday, I will not have time to do all that has to be done.

He said all right whenever you would like. It all right with him.

Wednesday afternoon four of my class mates from my school days come over to the house. We had a good time planning the garden party in a fortnight. This was so all of us can get to know the families of one another. When Jim come home that night the girls where about to depart they said there good nights after talking to Jim some saying we will see you at the party in a fortnight.

My heart is full of happiness, Jim is my man for ever and ever they can never be another that can take his place in my heart. Jim is so good and gentle. I'm in Jim's home and he is in my heart.

As will you know a tongue can cut deeper and sharper than any two edged sword. It can cut your heart open right to the inter most parts, with just one remark.

When I enter in to our courtyard I'm so embarrass and intimidated by the neighbor women. I feel self conscious by!

The neighborhood women call me a prostitute, saying I'm in that foreigners house and unmarried.

Stating we know your mother and father they are good people and good neighbors. Your parents are good they would never bring disgrace upon their home or their name. They would never disgrace the nighborhood they are good Japanese parents.

Not like you! and your foreigner. You are a big disgrace to all of us. Why don't you and your foreign lover just move away from heir? If Jim ever fond out about them I don't know what he would do. He would up hold the name of my family and beet the shit out of our neighbor men!

I just bow my head lower then they. Showing my embarrassment.

We are madly in love I just knew I would die with out my Jim.

This one night we walked up the hill just to pass the time away. Sit and look out over the bay and see the sun go down. When we arrived at the park, my mother and father where sating on a park bench. I went to the shrine to say my prayer for us. Then we went over to greet the family.

My mother and father knew that we are not married and that I am in this man's house living as man and wife.

I was so embarrass that they knew.

Mother welcome us as we walked up. But father just looked so angry!

He spoke in Japanses so Jim can't understand.

Saying "you must be out of your mind! That American will go home and you will never see him after that, Are you mentally ill or what? Your American!"

I sit there in disgrace, bowing my head in submission.

Thinking I'm so in love with Jim how can I tell father that I can't help my self. How can I make father understand.

I don't know, maybe I am insane like father said.

All I know is that I will kill my self if I never see Jim after he returns to the United States of America. I'm siting next to father there with my head bowed. I was to embarrass to look at father.

Father saying "What will you do when your American sailor returns to the United States of America!"

Mother said "**She will come back home!**"

We are speaking in Japanese so Jim don't know what is said.

But Jim is good at reading and understanding what's in your face. So he knew that father was mad as hell at me and him (over us).

After the sun was down and we arrived back home. We are in the kitchen it was around 8:00 p.m.

We are having a hot cup of tea. I was looking into my man's eyes thinking. My love I'll kill myself if you go away and never return to me.

Jim sit down his cup stood in front of me facing me. He is kneeling my hand in his.

Jim ask "would you be my wife? I'll be the best husband I can."

My heart is full of happiness it's about to jump out of my breast.

I said "**YES** my love. You have made me the happiest woman in the world. "O" yes; yes my love yes.

We kiss deeply time after time. Jim and I made love right there in the kitchen. Once on the kitchen table and then on the floor.

The next day after Jim went to work on the ship. I went to my parents house and told mother about Jim asking to marry him.

Mother ask "Have you two sit the date. Where the wedding going to be and what are you going to do if he returns to the states and don't take you. More over my little Kimiko what if he takes you to America we will never see you. For you are my baby girl forever. I know you love him but why couldn't you fill in love with a nice Japanese man so I can see you some time.

I think if you go to America I may never see you any more my little Kimiko."

I know I will never see any grandchildren. My Kimiko you know that your father and I love you so, we just want the best for you.

You go to your American and marry with him and have a good life with each other. I just hope I can see my grandchildren some day.

May GOD bless your Jim and you. Make me lots of grandbabies you come back home some time so I may see them."

Mother put her arms around me kiss me and pulling me closely to her she said in my ear "Good-by my baby girl good-by."

Then pulling away smiling said "hello young woman you have come to take my babies place in life."

"Mother, my dear mother I will love you and father forever but it is time for me to go from this time of my childhood and this place in life I must move on into womanhood. Mother I don't know the date and I do not know where. All I do know Jim ask me to marry him I said yes. Maybe we can have the wedding at our house, Jim's and mine. Our place has that big room on the side that no one ever uses. Mother all I know I am dancing on air. When I come back down from floating on the clouds I can think about all of that. Right now I'm out of my mind with happiness. Mother do you hear me I'm in love and I'm getting married. Come mother be happy and dance. Come on mother dance and be happy for me!"

Mother and I are hand in hand dancing around and around laughing, Dancing out the door into the yard.

Locus come running to see what was going on. Then brother and father all of us are laughing and dancing.

Locus saying "now Jim well fill that big house full of children." When Jim come home that evening I had a hundred question. What do we do about this or that?

Jim saying "your brother has not been married all that long. Why don't you go talk to your sister-in-law Locus and ask her to help you out."

I said "not to night, to night I just won't to be in your arms up next to you. Just lay by your side and love you. Never mined me I'm just in love that all."

After dinner we where in the big room. It was empty that make it look even bigger It was around 65 X 85 feet. I think some one said I don't know.

At one end there was a small family shrine the other end of the room there was no doors or windows just a wall. The back side of the room had seven windows and the front has the outer front has the walkway with twelve one the inside and twelve doors that can be open to the out side. The room it self can be separated into smaller rooms by using sliding doors. The floor are Tatami mats.

Jim and I was semi-dwarfed in the big empty room as we are hugging and kissing Jim is so huggable. Between kisses we are talking about what was facing us.

I was laying back looking up at the eighteen foot open beam ceiling. I ask my self how can I clean them beams.

Locus and Brother was at the door.

Jim calls out to them, "we are in the side room. Come on in you are welcome any time. You are all most family so pleas come on in make your self at home, my house is your house."

Locus and Brother entered the room. Locus seeing the gold inlaid shrine with the out side lamp through the window come dancing through on the inlay making golden ringlet that dances around the room.

Speaking in Japanese Locus ask "Is this the place you are going to have your wedding? It is big and it's beautiful.

Have you two set the date?

The family,

The gusts,

The invitation

and the food."

Locus was laughing and jumping with joy as she danced around and around the room.

Brother and Jim were just looking at her jumping with joy.

Jim said "I don't know what she is saying but she is happy what ever it is."

I said "she is planning the wedding for us. Here in this room. But we don't have a date."

Jim ask "what about May 15, it's a Friday and payday ever one will be happy that day we will all have money and time off the weekend what more can one need."

Now we have the time; the place and the date.

The next afternoon when Jim come from work. He said there will be 12 men from off the ship coming to the wedding.

That will be his best friends.

One will be the Caption of the Jupiter ship and the X. O.

and the 12 sailors that is 14 from Jim's side 18 friends and 15 family. totaling 47 It will be formal dress.

Jim and his friends will be in full dress whites with their shine golden swords and white gloves.

My father will give me away at our wedding. Father said "I not mad at Jim or you. He just asking over and over an American why? You know we will never see you after you go off with him."

The time and date 6:00 O'clock May 15, 1952 I'm in my mother old Japanese wedding dress.

I am up and dressed and looking like a ghost with all the powder and the big old time wig.

A little past 8:00 O'clock a. m. Locus was with me and she would say you look beautiful. Come now it is time to walk the neighborhood, in the old Japanese custom.

The bride and all her bride maids to walk in the streets with a drummer beating the drum to ward off evil spirits.

The children from the neighborhood shooting off fireworks. We are walking, ever one was laughing all in a joyful and happy mood all the people dancing as we pass by.

It was noon by the time we returned to the house.

Some of the guest had arrived for the wedding there was more laughing and talking some were dancing to the music played by the three piece band,

My heart was full of happiness I had tears in my eyes, tears of happiness.

Locus said "You just stop that right now. Before your make up gets all messiest up. So just stop it right now!"

When it was time to begin the wedding ceremont. All the guest are in the big room. The women with their nice dresses of all colors like flowers in from the garden. The Japanese men in there black.

The Americans in the Navy whites.

I looked in to see how things looked it was all so briefly looking. Just then the band begun the prologue to the wedding march.

As I enter the room. Ever eye was on father and I we entry at a half step. At the other side and other end of the room.

Jim was in his dress whites with his golden medals.

On one side the best man next to him. The minister then the bride maids.

Father and I arriving at Jim's side. Father places my hand into Jim's hand father then stepped back and a side.

We kneeled down in front of the minister to take our wedding vows.

When we arouse and stand in front of the minister he said you may kiss the bride.

Jim put his arms around me and pulling me close to him. I put my arms around him looking up in his face. He kissed me with along and deep so very soft like I was a delicate flower.

We departed out of a side door of the house through the garden with all the flowers.

The old gardener had it looking lovely all the flowers where so beautiful we stepped over to the main walkway to go out the gate.

The twelve sailors six on each side of the walkway next to the gate with there golden swords arched up over our heads.

Arm in arm we walked slowly under the arched swords.

Just out side the gate the newspaper reporters with there light bulb going off all over the place.

They ask about the wedding with a Japanese woman and a American man marring so close after the war?

What our two family's though about it?

After about ten times asking the same thing over and over Jim said to the reporters "get out of here!"

About that time the twelve sailors come running out the gate with their swords in hand and eight of them surrounding the auto and the other run after the reporters.

With the drummer beating the drum we walk down the street.

Two show ever one we are marred so no one will woman or man will flirt with us.

In the Japanese tradition with the drummer beating the drum.

The people on the side of the street the motor cars honking there horns. The fireworks going off and the neighborhood children running here and there.

The joyful people wound toss rice and lay flowers in the road for us to walk on.

When we returned to the house. The food and drank where ready.

The party was out in the garden

Jim and I cut the cake with Jim's sword. Jim said in my ear I never knew what I was to use that dam thing for, now I know it to cut wedding cakes.

We dances and had the wedding glass of wine.

The minister wrapped the wine glasses in a white cloth and laying them at our feet. For us to stomp on them and breaking the glasses when we did all the American clapped there hands and letting out a loud yell, with louder out cry of laughter.

We had a fortnight for our honeymoon.

Ever one was out by the motor car to see us off.

Jim knows more about Japan than I do. We stopped that night at a hotel over looking a beautiful lake near Fujiysan and staying for ten days.

We where out walking around looking the place over. They had this big shrine I went in and said a pray for Jim and I and our wedding. Jim never goes inside. This priest walked up to us. He was talking in English. I don't know what kind of priest he was.

He ask Jim if he was station here in Japan.

He said "one of you will have to gave up there way of life. For east is east and west is west, there are no half ways. I said "We are here at the hotel on our honeymoon. My husband is in the United States Navy. He will return to San Francisco, California and fines us a house in Alameda, California. I will go to Alameda to be with my husband."

I'm thinking to myself when that day comes for Jim to go States side. I will just up and die.

The priest was some what unexpectedly surprised.

He ask "you are going to the United States and leaving your life time friends?

What about your family, your mother and your father, wow about your sisters and brothers?

You may never see or hear from them.

Do you know that, have you though about that?

How will his family like having a damn Jap in the family?

Maybe some one of his family were killed in the war.

What if his father said take your Jap wife and got out and never come back? What do you think you would do?"

Jim said in return "That will never happen. But if it was to, but it never will happen. But if it did, I would have to say **(SAYONARA)** to all of them."

The priest said "I hope it will never come to that."

After the honeymoon was over and we are back home.

I showed no embarrassment whim I enter our courtyard Jim and mine. The first home my husband and I had. I can and I do face them the same neighborhood women with the satisfaction, knowing I have married the more excellent suitable and desirable and with a higher degree and a superior person.

Surpassing there lower life husbands.

Now I do not bow my head lower. Just the same now and some of the time I just a half a bow.

Make no mistake about my neighbor women for they are unfair and will take advantage of you if they can.

The day has come the one we knew would come some day. But not so quickly.

"NOT SO QUICK!"

Jim said "the Jupiter will sail for San Francisco at 0600 hours.

We did not sleep at all that night. Jim said it would take the old ship over 90 days to arrive in San Francisco. And for me to get a pass port and a Visa so when the ship arrives in Alameda he will rent a place for us.

At 0400 hours there come the knock on the door it was Jim's driver. Opening the door saying to the young driver I'll be right there with you. The driver ask "Your bags I'll put them in the car for you. If you need me just call I'll be at the car.

Jim kiss me good by then once more. He was out the door and into the waiting naval car.

As they drove off down the hill, maybe I'll never see my Jim again.

Had father been right all the time? 'O' no not Jim I knew my husband, he will return to me I just know!

The days pass so slowly like each day has 48 hours in one day.

As the days turned slowly in to weeks and the weeks turn slowly in to months. GOD knows how I have a desire to be in his arms.

My heart is broken! What can I do? It has been two and half months. I ask did you do what father said you'll do.

Chapter Three

From Kimiko

'**O**' Jim, my Jim, I need you so!

I can't sleep! I can't eat!

All I won't is to see you Jim, the love of my life for you are my life. Without you I have no life.

You said it would be around 90 days before he would be in port at Alameda, California and it has been 73 days.

I have a fortnight to go.

The next day August 24,1950. Locus come running to my house saying "Kimiko

Kimiko come to mother house it's Jim on the telephone."

I run as fast as my legs would take me. Picking up the telephone and saying "Jim my lover it has been a life time. Are you all right" Brother said you have to say over. So I said over.

Jim answered in return "Yes I'm all right. How are the others and how is grandmother?

I did not think this old ship was ever going to get to Alameda, over.

I said I have the pane of happiness in my heart. Just to hear you on the telephone, over.

Jim said "Come to San Francisco for I love you more than life itself. I can't be without you my love.

You have your passport go get a 30 day vacation visa, take the plane to San Francisco.

You phone me here on the ship before you get on the plane.

Ask the duty officer of the day for me if I'm not there you ask the duty officer his name.

You write it down so you can give it to me. Give him the time your plane will arrive in San Francisco airport and the flight number.

I'll phone you ever day till you are in my arms, over.

What do you need in the way of Passport and Visa ? Go to the Bank. You keep a million yen or more whatever you think, you will need for the plane and whatever you need. Transfer the remainder to our bank in San Francisco. Get all the money out.

When you hand in your paper work for your visa have a twenty thousand yen note clipped to the paper, over."(20,000yen=$55.56) On the second day when Jim telephoned stating he received the message with the flight number and time.

Mother has been grieving for the passed week knowing I was going to San Francisco. She keeps saying "My little girl is going to America I will never see her again in addition I know I will never see my grandchildren. My little Kimiko why can you have marred a Japanese man so you would not move where I'll never see you."

Father just said "I had hoped you would not marred your American so we could have keep you a little longer. But you have and the sorrow in my hart. I can see is small, next to the love you show for your American. So go with God and be happy with your American. His name is Jim and he is from Kansas state. It is time for my little bird to fly away. If you return it will be with sad hart and open arms, to your return."

Brother and his wife said "Good luck and be happy. Come home if you can to see the family. You know that would make the family happy,"

The family seen me off at Tokyo airport.

When I arrived at San Francisco airport. I had departed Tokyo on a Monday. Got in to San Francisco Monday afternoon.

Crossing the enter national date line.

When I disembarked the plane I seen Jim.

Dees and a woman was there too great me. The woman was Dees new wife, she was from Texas also like Dees. We drove to Alameda in Dees auto where Jim had rented us an apartment,

The first night after three months without my husband; We made love all night did not sleep at all that night.

The first weekend that Jim was off duty we drove to Reno, Nevada,

We got remarried in the states. Jim said "It was for the nary they need a certificate of our marriage he did not want to use ours before some one miss place it." They need it so I can get paid and receive my benefits and a Navy I. D. card. He said it all about finances you know. But I did not that was all right. Dees and his wife was there at the wedding. Our room was beautifully appointed not luxury but nice.

Dees and his wife had drove use up to Reno. Dees had to report back for duty on Monday. We come back to Alameda that Sunday afternoon.

We had been in our small apartment just over a fortnight, and this one day in the mid afternoon. Jim come running into the apartment like the house was on fire. He was laughing; full of joy as he kept saying over and over. Going to Texas **No more loving ships!**

Picking me up off my feet and swing me around and around singing. You're my yellow rose of Texas. After saying we are going to Texas over and over a good ten more times. He said "I got my orders to V. T. 27 at Naval Air Station Corpus Christi, Texas. I don't even know where Corpus Christi is at. All I know is there know loving ships their."

He received his orders and departed the U. S. S. Jupiter (AVS-8) he was so happy to get off that ship.

We had 35 days before we had to report for duty.

Jim's old motor car a 1940 Ford may not make it out of Alameda.

I know it'll never run the 1,800 miles to Corpus Christi, Texas. Jim said that old Ford will run for ever.

In the City of Cambria, California FOR EVER COME.

The old motor car stopped running. We got a room for the night.

Jim said we can have it repaired the next day when the shops open.

Now I just knew Jim was nuts! Here we are in the middle of GOD only knows. The motor car will not run. We have 1,800 miles before we get to Texas.

I have not seen Jim so damn happy, for some time.

There was more loving then sleeping them two days and nights. We did not leave that room.

Jim said "The damn old car will not run, what more can we do."

The third day he had the car repaired. We drove all night the next day we stopped and got a room them drove all day and night we arrived at Taso, New Mexico. At his brothers place. Now this is New Mexico not old Mexico. Where is old Mexico ?

I was saying that his place was big land, they all laughed at that.

Jim said this is just a big back yard, it's just 38 acres that is small out here in New Mexico.

The next day Jim and his brother come to the house on horse back with two other horses. Jim's sister-in-law said come on Kimiko we can all go for a horseback ride.

I said "O" no! I have never been on a horse before in my life. Jim's brother said "That's all right this horse has never been rode before." Jim dismounted his animal, coming over saying it will be all right we'll be riding slow. Come put your foot in the stirrup. Your hands up here and pull your self up in to the saddle. Keep your feet firmly in the stirrups. Did what Jim said to do and got on.

About that time Bob's horse leap into the air. As they rushed a cross the yard leaping in the air. Jim's brother punches the horse in the head and cursed him.

The animal realize the rider was fearless. Bob said that is about all he will do he'll be all right now.

We rode up into the hills and returning back as the sun was going down. Jim and his brother put the horses up. His sister-in-law said us have a Bar-B-Q I said all right thinking for just the four of us. However she went in to the house and made some phone calls and in a hour there was pickup trucks and big cars and small ones in the drive way and out on the street. Ever one had food, some of them had violins, banjos and other stringed instrument. The party was on. Music and dancing, food on the Bar-B-Q.

Ever one of them had a fire arm and they all removed them putting them by the door.

Jim was back from putting up the horses. Bob removed his gun and put it with the others. After the party was slowing down. A old man got to his feet with violin in hand ever one stopped to hear him play. He played the sweets music I think I have here heard when he stopped playing. There was not a dry eye in the place.. Then he begun playing a fist song and the others joined in and after that the old man come over and said Hi to us.

Bob said this is not a Texas Bar-B-Q out here in New Mexico are some what reserved.

The women helped clean up and by 10:30 you would never knew a party had been here.

The hair raising horse back ride, the Bar-B-Q and all them guns ever one up their got one or two.

The music and dancing. I sleep good that night.

The next day we drove all day the sun had sat by the time we arrived at Jim's home. North west of Caldwell, Kansas.

Jim's father was coming in from his milking.

He was so happy to see us, he put his arms around Jim and saying

"Welcome home my boy. This must be Kimiko?"

Putting his big arms around me and giving me a welcome kiss on my cheek.

Calling out "Mother come and see who is here!"

She come to the back door and seen us and come running to welcome us she was so happy to see us and kissing each of us. She said the periodical son has returned home we will have a partyfor him. Like in the Bible."

The next day after Jim's father did the milking we sit and talked most of the day. Mid afternoon Jim's farther said he had some farm chores to tend too. Saying he had to move the beef animals to the south field.

Jim said "Dad let Kimiko and me do that for you. So she can see some of the farm." We went out to a old farm truck that looked older that I was. Jim drove off like a bat out of hell, out past some big farm buildings. Out into a open field stretching out as far as you can see we are out around 300 yards from the buildings.

Jim stop the truck got out saying it is time you know how to drive.

I said "Are you crazy, I don't know how to drive this truck."

He said "now is the time for you to drive or walk, Just that it is a good time.

I put my hands on the wheel stepping down on the gas and a cross the field we go. Jim would say turn right and turn left or stop and go by the time we got to the other side of the field I can stop about where I won't to.

We come to a gate that went into another field. Jim got out and open the gate I drove through the gate and stopped for Jim to close the gate.

When he got in he said "I'll make a old farm girl out of you yet;"

Driving through this field it had trees and grass.

The next field was where the beef cow were at.

I stopped at the gate Jim got out and open the gate, I drove through and stopped for Jim. Jim come running got in the truck about that time all the cows come up around the truck putting their heads in side of the trucks window.

I screamed! Screaming Jim! Jim "O" shit what do I do now!

That big cow is going to eat me. Jim what am I to do?

Jim was laughing so hard. I would of like to have punches his lights out. "Jim you S. O. B.! What are we going to do!"

Jim bent over and honk the horn the cows moved away. We moved them to the other field.

He said this is the feeder truck they were just after some thing to eat. I said "Yes me."

Jim had to laugh some more. Said "They just eat grass, and one or two times a year a little Japanese woman farmer."

I was mad saying "You asshole you could have told me we are driving the feeder truck. Them damn cows scared the shit out of me you asshole!"

After Jim looked the waters over we got back in to the truck.

Jim ask "do you wont to go back on the road?"

I said I can't drive on the road.

Jim said "I can't has never done a damn thing in all his life.

I can't.

Have you ever tried to?

No you have not so go for it baby just go for it."

I drove to the gate Jim got out and open it I drove through and stopped. Jim got back into the truck and I drove out on to the road. On the road back to the house I would run off the roar.

Jim would just say "when you get tired of driving in the drainage ditch you can get back on the road."

I run off the road two more times after that. As I turned into the driveway;

I turn too much and went up into the garden, Jim just turn off the key and the truck stopped. Jim said "Now think of what you are going to do. Restart the truck and back out of the garden."

I did and backed out of the garden on to the driveway and drove on into the yard, stopped and turning off the key. As we got out of the truck.

Jim said "You did good, you never run over any one." He went to help his Dad with the chores.

I went in the house, my mother-in-law ask me all about Japan and if I liked it here in the States.

I said "I love it here, Jim is so good to me. He just beats me one or two times a week is all." My mother-in-law eyes got small and you could see the anger in her eyes. Then she was happy one more saying you got me that time.

I said "It would be nice to see my mother and father."

She ask if I had any brothers or sisters.

Yes one brother no sisters. He works with our father in the family business. Never said what that business was, She never ask.

Ever day Jim would say you drive and we'll go water the cattle. He said the livestock needs some one to look after them ever day. One good milk cow will use up to 38 gallons of water in one day.

He said "To night when we go milk, you come with me. I'll milk the cows, and you can milk the steers.

I said "O. K." Jim was smiling at me as we drove a cross the wheat field. I stopped the truck at the first gate Jim open the gate and I drove through when he got back in he had that shit eating smile.

I said "What?" "Why are you smiling at me that way?"

Jim said "Honey you don't milk all the livestock on the farm. First you have the bull he is the butterfly going from one to the other. He the Ichiban to all the cow's or any females. Then there the heifers a young maybe one year old female. The mama milk cows are the older ones. You have the steers they are the young males with his testicles removed. The older steer are called an oxen are older with there testicles removed, cut off as a baby. So they will get bigger you work them like you would a workhorse. The beef yearly are the same but they don't make it through there second year. When we arrived at the field that the livestock where. Jim showed me the bull he was a noble looking animal. He had the biggies testicles I have ever seen. Jim checked on the water and looking at the field, the grass was still up to the knees, then he said "Us go on back. Do you wont to go on the road or cross the field ?""The road, yes I think I can keep it on the road this time." We come up over a small hill and a car was coming. He said just pull over in to the ditch and stop. We will let the car go past us. The other car stopped beside us. The young woman driver said "Hi, I heard you was back. Is this your wife Kimiko, it must be, that your mother toll me about".

Jim said "Yes this is my wife Kimiko. Kimiko this is our neighbor three miles over to the west of us this is Joann, Kimiko Joann.

Joann Kimiko." There are our next door neighbor over to the west of us.

We have just been over to the southeast field looking at Dad's cattle.

She said it's nice to meet you. You two will have to stop by before you go back to the navy, "as she drove off down the road. I drove the truck back up on the road and go on the Jim's Dad place.

Jim said "her brother and I went to Kansas State."

That evening my mother=in-law said "come and go with me we'll go out and see the men milking."

I tolled her about Jim saying He would milk the cows and I could milk the steers. She smiled and said "That my Jimmy boy all right." We arrived at the barn it was bigger then it looked from the out side. It was two story building on the side where we come in there was storage rooms, one was full of barley, one with oats, and one had corn the other had wheat for the animals. That cover about half of the east side of the barn. The other half of the east side was for horses.

In the middle of the barn was hay stacked up about 15 or 16 feet high. On the west side of the barn was where the milk cows are milked. They use a milking machine 4 cows at one time.

There was the other milking barn on the other side of the barn yard that is not been used any more. As they don't have all the work horses to work the fields any more. After the milking was completed for the night and milking machine cleaned up.

Jim and I went up to the top of the hayloft it was all most to the top with baled hay. Jim said come on up to the top of the hay. Stepping from one bale to the other climbing to the top, walking over the top of the hay.

I ask "Are the cattle going to use all of this in just one year?"

Jim taking my hand and pulling me down beside him, Kissing me putting his hands under my brassiere exposing my naked breasts. He was kissing my breasts.

I said "stop it your mother and father are down their working. What if they come up here."

He said they have gone on up to the house by this time. Come on this will make you a good old Kansas country girl out of you.

With his other hand he unzipped my blue jeans sliding them down, taking my under garment off with my jeans. He would suck my tongue deep into his mouth I just love it when he suck my tongue into his mouth, it makes me go insane. I lost it, when fe did that.

Jim ask "are you all right?"

"Yes just a minute I'm all right."

When he inter me I'll be damn if I went off right then and their. We rolled around in the hay all night he was doing ever then just right.

Now stop and think about it, here I am bare ass naked in a hayloft with this insane country boy. Having sexual intercourse and loving ever minute of it,

After that night will I can say I'm a good old Kansas country girl.

Just running bare ass naked over that hay turn me on that night and Jim said letter "that it was the best sex he ever had."

I know it was the best sex I have ever had in my life.

It come time we have to go on to Texas.

We stopped at his sisters house in Dallas to see her. She had to work the next day so we went on to Corpus Christi.

The next day we arrived in the city of Corpus Christi, Texas.

We moved into a small apartment.

Tell the base housing had us a house.

We hadsome time before Jim had to check in for duty.

97

We would drive around sit seeing Out onto the Naval Air Station seen the air craft of VT 27.

One day we where out driving a round. I ask "Jim a garage, that is the house for the car right?"

Jim said yes that a garage for the car.

I ask "why are they selling there garage?" Jim ask "What are you saying." I said "LOOK their GARAGE SALE did you see the sign?" He stop at the next one of the signs and showed me that what a garage sale was.

Jim reported for duty in VT 27 at Naval Air Station Corpus Christi. Texas.

We lived in Corpus Christi for a long time just under 10 years. In July we had our first child in the Naval Air Station Hospital wenamed her Lyn.

Jim thinks I got pregnant here in Corpus Christi. But I know it was in that damn hayloft in Kansas. I just know. Women know about things like that. I know it was all most nine months to the day.

I'm here to tell you, I'm not about to go up into a hayloft with this insane sailor again. (Tell the next time)

Jim sold the old Ford and got a used one year old Cadillac. Saying when in Texas do as the Texan do. Now this was a big car with room to move around in.

Now you know my nutty Jim. He said it was good luck to make love in the new car.

Will don't you just know it in August James JR.

Jim got a new 1957 Cadillac.

November 21, 1958 Andrew. Yes the 57 had room in it to move around in also. I become an American citizen and changed my name to Kim. No more Kimiko it's just Kim from now on.

I got my driver license and a check book with my name on it. My Mother become ill and was in hospital. The doctor said "She mite pass away.

We did not have the money for me to fly home. Jim went to work at a off duty second job. He worked hard for six weeks working day and night ever hour he was off duty.

I was in need of my American pass/port and with a Japanese visa before I can go. He got the money for the plane and I received the American passport but I had not received my Japanese visa, I telephone my father to see how mother was doing.

Father said "She was a lot better now with the new medicine. She was out of hospital and home. She is out in the yard walking right now. She walks each day, here she is now." I ask "Mother what happen? Are you working to hard? You have to stop doing hard work. Locus would do the house work if you would permit her to. She can do the cooking as well." Mother said "I well be all right I just got the wrong medicine was all." I said "Jim has just received his orders to Iwakuni, Japan, that is just on the other side of Hiroshima. I can come to see you ever day if need be. It will be about four months before we see you, Good by for now we'll see you soon."

The new over seas telephone now you don't have to say over when you stop talking. We had three babies at Corpus Christi Naval Air Station Hospital. I be come an American citizen.

Jim got us a new Ford motor car. Saying the Cadillac was to old to take to Japan.

This one night, Jim and I where out on Padre Island. This road that went up into the sand dunes there's a parking lot. We are the only car around, Jim and I are in the middle of blessing the new car.

When a park policeman shining his bright light in on our nakedness.

He turned off his bright light and said "Damn I gave a hard time of keeping the teenagers ran out of here. You two are older couple know better. Now get the hell out of here before I run you in and your children have to come and get you two out of jail." We put on our close and drove out as quick as we could.

The children are happy they don't have school tell next year. They'll miss some school.

Jim has 90 days of school in Califorña at Moffitt Field, California. We had a nice time in California. The children like swimming ever day, and no school. Daddy had to go to school.

After Jim completed his schooling to brang him back to speed after ten years in a training command.

He said he need the schooling before reentering the fleet command. With the new aircraft, new engines, new tools that are helpful, and all types of new items, after being out of the fleet for so long.

We had rented an apartment in Milpitas, California.

The apartment was up on the side of a hill, and from the second floor bedroom window we had a view, over looking the south bay.

On the weekends we would take the children to San Francisco zoo and the parks, and other places that children like to go

We would see Jim's Aunt she could speak Japanese some of the time she would make me laugh the way she would go on about the people and the tribes on the island that keep them in the hills so the Japanese army could not find them, John and her.

She said that they sleep and eat with the hills tribes.

It had been a long time ago and her Japanese was not right all the time. She has a nice home in San Leandro, California.

After Jim had completed his schooling we turn in our automobile to be shipped to Japan. We used one of Aunt's auto for three days.

She drove us to the ship in San Francisco.

I was sicker than two dogs all the way over to Japan, sea sick I was so nauseated by the motion of the ship. The Doctor gave me a shoot but that did not work. So I stead in bed all the way over.

We docked in Japan and went to Tachikawa Air Base.

We take the train to Yokosuka then a taxi onto mother and father's house. We stayed a fortnight.

My mother looked so older than my father, and father is five years older. My daddy was so happy to see his grandchildren, Jr. and my father hit it off at the first. Daddy would take Jr. to the store, on the way he would tell to all the neighbors. "This is my grandson from America." Mother and father was so happy to see all of us.

Jim ask me if my father still would like to kill him? I said no but I'm thinking about it. But you are my good lover so you are alright for now.

This one afternoon father said "Kimiko I'm so happy for you that I was mistaken about your American. We miss you so. But to see you two so happy with each other and the children so nice and they are happy, Your mother and I will have to step a side and let you go on with your American."

I said "Thank you mother and daddy, thanks. You know I'm still as much in love with my American. As I was when that young and foolish girl become a woman in his arms over 11 years ago. Father place forgave me for disobeying you.

But I was and still am so much in love with Jim. I just had to see him, father can and will you forgave me."

Father said I have a hundred times. You know all we wonted was the best for our little girl. We did not won't her to grow into womanhood.

Yes I know but Jim and the children are my life now and I must go with my family where ever they go, I must go.

One afternoon Locus and I was talking about how time had changed us over the years.

How Brother and her had lost interest in the sexual desire and did not make love like they did when they paid special attention to one another's needs. With out getting the attention, time has faded his sexual desires. I said Now Jim has this old American saying; (Woman who keeps man in dog house; Will find him in cat house,) "NOW you and only you can stop it. Don't allow it to happen to your marriage. Locus you know the Japanese way to keep your man happy! Will I'm here to tell you there is more to it than that.

In the morning before he goes to work you make him a good breakfast. Do your hair, maybe some makeup and a nice kimono that is open just a little more than proper. Make him get the message, you are the best lover he will ever come across in his life time. You need to be skillful.

Be aware of his physical emotion. Other than saying, No don't do that. Or I'm not about to do that. You see you are in control, the dominating one without him knowing it. It is your job to make him think he is more and than you will ever know or ever wont. Let him eat you out if he would like to. Or you can eat him if you would like to. Do whatever the two of you like. Let him do it dog style. I said "As for me I know Jim is the only man I will ever need

Just to think of sleeping next to some other than Jim makes my skin craw. Shit; If I'm ever without him. No I mean no man will ever take his place. He has me so fucked up I'll kill myself if he was ever to leave me for another woman. However these days-or a man. We are like two people in one."

I said "Locus you two do whatever you won't to. Fear not what others say. If you have a request you would like ask him to do it, whatever it is, Whatever the two of you like or need to be happy in the bedroom, It's all up to the two of you. But Locus you have to take the first step."

That Monday, Tuesday and Wednesday Brother did not go to work. They never come to the main house to eat. Thursday after Brother left for work. I seen Locus outside there small house that sit near the back of the court yard.

Locus said "Kimiko you were right! Just some good old deranged sexual intercourse was what was needed. He did not won't to go to work today.

But I toll him; I'll be right here for you when you come home." She was her old self the Locus I knew before. She was happy once more.

Locus said "I just let him do what ever he liked. Some of the things he wonted was the back door, I said I like the dog. I more than made it up to him in other ways.I used the feather on him. So I started to have oral sex on him. At first he did not know what to think about me, doing him like that running my tongue all around the head of it and put it all the way in my mouth, I put my hands on the back of his head and moved him down on me. We had oral sex, I though he was going to keep going till I die. That is the way I won't to go. Straight sex over and over he just coming back for more.

Do you and im ever have oral sex" I said "No we are to straight, about all he likes to suck my breast and run his tongue a round the nipples. That is about all we need."

Locus said "think you for he;ping me out for I don't know what I would have done."

It had come time for the children, Jim and me to go on down to Iwakuni. For it was about time for him to report for duty.

The first night we stayed at the base lodge the first night that was not for us.

I ask around about a house off base. One was for rent about one mile from the main gate. We went over and looked at it. A brown stone two story with a front yard, it had three bedrooms up top and one bigger one on the first floor. A hot tub and three other rooms we did not use. After our things come in we used the front room for the front room. The other side room was for the children to play in. The small back room we eat in. After we got the off base house. Jim reported for duty at the Power Plant shop, N. A. S. U. at M. C. A. S. Iwakuni, Japan.

He come home the first day and just said "I have a shop full of assholes working for me. But that is all right, I'm not on some loving ship." He never did say any more about them.

On the weekends we would drive to Hiroshima (40 miles) and take the Friday night drive on ferryboat to Yokohama and motor on to Yokosuka to see family that would be one or two times a month. One weekend at my parents house, some one said Jim and my old house was for sale. Jim and I walk over just ti look at the place. The first home my husband and I loved and lived in.

Jim ask me if I wonted to live here after he retired. We can you know. I'll have my navy retirement pay we can live on.

I said "No this is not my home any more. The children and I all live in the United States we are all Americans now just like my husband. It is just nice to look back in time over the years that has past us by."

I asked "Are you seeing the two young lovers kissing in the shadows under that big tree. Do you?"

Jim said "Yes I do ever time I look at you my love of my life. I see the most beautiful young Japaese woman that I have ever seen sitting under that tree she was with a ugly American who will marry her and make her so unhappy all her life."

I said "My love place don't do that you know I wont to kiss your lips off your face when you say thing like that."

The weekend had ended and we are back at Iwakuni. Jim received a phone call from the housing office to come in to the office. They had us a house in side the gate. When Jim arrived some upper officer, was giving the housing officer hell for not having him a house. The housing officer gave Jim the eye not to say any thing.

The housing Officer said "I do have one house I was going to rent to this Jr. Officer but if you wont a house today, right now you can rent this one." El/shit head saying "yes I do ; I'm higher than you navy officer!" At that, he departed the office. The housing officer said "That assholes house would have been readied in two days.

Here the address drive by and look at it. Think you would wait two more days for this one. Over the one I gave El/shit head.

We moved into the base housing it had five bedrooms and three water closets. With a three car garage.

The children's school was just down the street they don't have to cross any streets. Jim walks to work. Som times when he comes home to eat at noon he'll drive a navy car or truck.

That's when he is out at the collection of mathematical elements area. Or as his workers call it (The Hot Spot) they run the motors up to 105% if they are good they go to supply if not they go back to the states.

He is happy in his work he has a crew two seven men. Steveson has crew one with seven men also.

Steveson son had training wheels on his bicycle. One day Steveson removed the training wheels, his son come up to my two boys and stopped with out putting his foot down. He fell off his bicycle and into the open shit ditch. He went home and said my boys put him in it. Steveson and Jim went to wor over that. But after aweek or so the Steveson boy toll he fell in and my boys had not put him in it.

Steveson had to go back to the States went into hospital.

The women next door on either side of us where nice, and I likewise to them. WE would have a meeting once a week at the neighbor that lives next door to the right side. She would teach the bible. I liked to go and hear about GOD and his son.

The neighbor on the other side of us would have tea in the afternoon but the older women would put whiskey in there tea cup.

I would go to her afternoon tea party it was her social gathering. So I would go just to be nice to her. Herhouse back door was on the side of our house. So we did not see one another that often. Some times her husband would send a car for her it had a red with three white stars on it. The flage was on the front mud guard.

Our other next door neighbor our houses sit side by side. Mary is a christian in the Church of the Nazaren. Mary knew the missionary Brother Gease. After some time, Jim and I with the children would go to church on Sunday. It was in town. They would be from one hundred to one hundred and twenty five Americans that come.

It was in English. Five to seven Japanese would come also. Mary has a small Japanese car that can go down the little side streets.

Our American Ford was to big we can't go down the side streets the streets are to small.

Mary ask us to go with her she could driver her small Japanese car right up to the churchs front door.

The American missionary 0t the Nazaren church. Ever one called him brother Gazze. Him and Jim become good friends. Some times we would motor to other city's for the day. Brother Gazze liked our Ford it was bigger than other cars in Japan Brother Gazze liked that. We would motor to places like Yamaguchi, Shimonseki. Tokuyama had a large zoo. The children liked to go to the zoo in Tokuyama. We motored to Kure and Hiroshima. They have a piece park at ground Zero where the first (A-Bomb) was explored helping to end W. W. II.

The place Jim and I liked was Miyajima a most beautiful Iland in the inland sea. Noted for it's shrine, built on supports running out into the sea. The small deer would eat out of your hand the the biggest one I seen was about 2 ½ to three feet high, and around six five to seven five pounds. No motor cars can come on to the Iland.

One of Jim's men was going home. So Jim got his old Japanese car It was older than dirt and just as pretty to look at. Jim paid twent five dollars for it. We never drove it out and around it was to old. It was A Suzuki motor car. Outside under the two doors where all bent up with holes. Jim said that gave it class. We name her Suz.

If it was raining or stormy he would drive it to work. In the evening after a bad day at work. He would drive out to the zoo. He did not won't to bring home all the stress and the mental tension.

The city zoo all the animals had the run of the place,

He would hand feed the small deer and the fishes and the monkeys was on a Iland so he would throw the food over to them. They had a jackass pined up like he has King Kong. The deer would see Jim drive up in Suz and come up to the car looking for there food.

After about one hour in the zoo with the animals he would be tranquil once more. The animals was running out no pen had the run of the zoo. But they would stay in the zoo.

Jim said "Suz is getting old and we can go only ten kilometers away from home. We can walk back home if we have to.

Spring time in Japan

Japan is the most beautiful in the spring the time with the cherry budding and blossom out all over.

Cherry blossom festival is a time for merry making celebration ½ the night. It is a time for the small children and young lovers to be happy.

We would go down to the river that run into the in land sea by the old foot bridge. The children would have candle stick on small boats and in the evening they would lit the candles and put them in the river as the small boats was going down the river it looked like thousands of fireflies dancing in the night.

On the weekends we would ride our bicycles around the city down by the river and over the foot paths. All the land has waken the green leaves with flowers ever place. To top it all off was the cherry trees with there beautiful flowers budding out.

Andrew was in kindergarten he said "He did not wont to go to school." I ask him why, you liked it the first part of the year. He said Miss. Michaset is mean to him, and the other kids. She will pinch me on the hand and thumps my head. Jim ask "what about the other children in your class?"

Andrew said "Yes and Jean cries when Miss Michaset pinches her." Jim ask the names of the other children. Jim was in the school in no time. He phone seven of them and they said yes there children toll the same stories.

Jim ask them if they would repeat there stories to the school board. Five of them said they would be most happy to. The next day the head of the school board phone Jim at his work and said "If you make this an official complaint we will have to let her go. She will have to go back to the states. Her husband is here

109

on the base and has one more year to go." Jim said "Just how official do you wont it I have others that well make a complaint. I wont that woman out of here today." He said if we let her go she will have to go back to the states. Jim said "So she needed to think about that before now. To day if not I'm going to the C.O. and have the others to make a official complapnt. Also of the school board knowing about her and sit on your hands. You may be out looking for a job."

The next day Andrew come home from school happy saying Miss Michaset had to go home to see her mother. The new teacher is nice to all of us.

One day Jim said we found air tools in a back room and ask one of the men that been here along time. Why are we not using they air tools. He said the officer of the shop don't let us use them. Jim said Go get our men and hand them out. He said the shop Officer is going to be mad as hell. About the time Jim got to the working floor, The shop officer come out of his office. Saying who in the hell said you can use them air tools. Jim said "I said to use them." You can't use air tools they will round off the nuts. Jim may I see you in my office? Once in side and the door closed away from the men.

Jim informed him all the nuts on the engine are steel locking and are one time usages. So how in hell are they going to fuck up the nuts on that engine? We can do the job in half the time. The man hours will more than make up for any nuts being rounded off.

You know when I got here it was three days from the engine shipping can to A. M. D. supply. I have cut that time down to one day.

After six years we departed Japan. Jim's department the men in power plant shop gave us a going away and retiring party all rolled up in one. The NASU commanding officer (C. O.) gave a speech it was one of them at/boys speeches. Ask Jim to say a word to the men.

Jim said "As will all of you know I have never been speechless in my life. However, speaking to you men to night. You sailors of Naval Air Supply Unit. It's like saying good by to one of my children. We worked side by side this 6 years. Some good men have gone to the States before me and some of you remain behind to do the hopeless never ending, thankless duty to GOD and country. Some times one needed's 26 hours in a day to just keep up with the fleet. To keep the aircraft in the air.

As I depart N. A. S. U. I leave behind the best men the United States Navy has.

My family and I are going to retirement we say to all of you who have split a knuckle on that colder then hell day. We say to all!"

Domo Arigato and Sayonara.

(Thank you very much and Good-bye)

When we departed Japan, my Parents had past a way. Now there is just Brother that remains in Japan.

Brother said on the day we got on the plane

"Locus and I will have to come to the States some time to see all of you."

I knew and he knew also when he said it, they would never come over to see us.

As I sit here in the plane before we left.

I said my good bys.

Good by my most loving Mother. I'll miss you dear Mother.

Good by my loving Fater good by.

Good by Brother you and I know we will never see one another any more.

Good by my life long girl friend Locus, look after Brother.

I said good by to my Japan, for ever.

Bowing my head I say

"Sayonara Japan good by."

I'll never see you again.

"I'll say sayonara,

I'll never more see you.

I'll say good by, Good by Japan."

The children saying "Don't cry Mama be happy we are going back home to the States."

Jim saying "Come children, leave your Mother alone so she can say her good by to her past and her home land."

The family Jim and I arrived back in California in time to enroll the children in school, in San Leandro, California.

Chapter Four

From Kimiko

My time come for me to report to the naval base Treasure Inland the shit hole of the west. When I checked in for retirement school. The man said the next class don't start for two weeks and its a 90 day class. Your transfer date is in 15 days. He said I don't know what to do, He phone the DOD and ask. He come back to me and ask me if I had a telephone said "Yes I do the number is LO-8-7067." He said call him before 0800 hrs.(8:00 am) every day and not to come in. He would tell me if they needed me. So I was free for the two weeks before I went to the Fleet reserves. After not having a job after 22 and half years I went looking for a place of business after three days I liked this Texaco out in Union City on Mission Blvd. and Appian Way it had three bays and two inlands with good in and out driveways and the owner wonted out. I was going to run it like a mom/ pop place. At the time we opened I had customer asking if I would do work on auto's. Money is money I said I would so within 60 days I had three men working in automotive repair with 6 men up front two at a time open 24 /7 two after school boys they were on from 3 pm to 6 pm. It got out I would replace a water pump on the Cadillac for $150.00 and parts. It would take all day to do one. I think I replaced ever Cadillac water pump in the east bay. Just to get into the water pump, one had to remove the radiator, air compressor, P/S, P/B, P/S/T, Gen. braces. Now you can see the water pump. A Cadillac pull in for gas I run into the back room. When we was in Taxes, Kimiko drove my Cadillac but moving around she had stopped driving. I got her

113

an old Cadillac and she drove it for some time. One day the old man I got the car from come in as if I would sell him the old Cadillac. He was driving a two year old Cad. I said "I'll tread even up car for car." He said done. Now Kimiko has got a newer car than my old Ford.

Pet Lewis the plant superintendent for Heckett Engineering. He was in for gas. The Texaco sales representative. Was angry, he wanted me to use all Texaco T.B.A. (tires, batteries, accessories) I said NO: no way am I going to do that. I use Penn's oil not Texaco oil. He ask way? I said Texaco oil is no fucking good! (I said that just get his goat.) Texaco oil is just as good as the other oil. On ever can of oil it has what in it on the top of the can. Like ss/sl ss/aa/tt and more. The batteries come from a store down Mission Blvd. they have the batteries before I get the old one out. As for the accessories the same store. As for the tires come from you. There $1000.00 up there I can't give away. The Texaco sales drove off angry as hell. Pet Said I need a man to drive if you ever need a job. I said I may just take him up on that. Sixty 60days later when Texaco come out for me to sing up for three more years. I said no think you, in the first place your sales rep. and me are like two cats and dogs. In three year we had Money to get the home in Union City we lived in for 40 years. I worked for Pet E. Lewis for about five years. Heckett Engineering Co. was Div. of Harsco Corp closed plant 21. We all out of work, I went to driving a Vin for Fidelity National Title the manager name was Tataina L. Dail. Before National I drove for V.I.P. Title then Fidelity National Title Co. Got V.I.P. and I come to work for National. I had a office and five men working for me. But what angry the hell out of me has the way they fired you. At 5:00 PM Friday they would say don't come to work Monday you are Fired: that was it. So I said to me when I leave this place Friday I just don't show up Monday. So when Pinkerton Said "Come on down we got more work than man power." Comes Friday I said to my 5 men (not good-bye see you Monday) but see you around.

I worked for Pinkerton for 12 years to make sergeant at 15 years I went in to hospital and did not work after that. By that time the kids were all marred or moved out. My daughter Lyn was marred a year after she got out of school. Mr. J.R. moved to Newark. Andrew was marred and it was just Kim and at home in a four bed room home. Sometime after was when we moved to Oregon. We were happy there, then Kim got down sick. Then Kim pass-a-way 1/17/2004. On that day you could say my life was over also. I moved back to California in with Lyn in Patterson A small farming town. Yes "O" God do I miss my Kimiko ever day/ ever night I don't won't to go, or do anything. It has been over nine years now and I would like God to take me. I'm 80 years old and time for me to see my Kimiko.

SAYONARA

The End

Printed in the United States
By Bookmasters